Praise

"Erotic Horror at its finest... *A Thing Divine* doesn't shy away from the steam or the gore. In fact, it combines the two, and managed to be hotter than expected. Fans of dark romance and horror will be very happy with this bloody and sensual story."

— BROOKLYN ANN, AUTHOR OF THE BRIDES OF PROPHECY SERIES

"With its shrewd, cutting prose and heavy dose of horror, *A Thing Divine* is a sultry, gothic, and dark romance that doesn't flinch away from being bloody and gruesome to show the true extent of the characters' all-consuming obsession and depravity. The sensual vampirism doesn't mean we can't also get a heavy helping of visceral carnality. Highly recommended for fans of erotic horror who enjoy vampires with both a romantic and monstrous streak."

— MORGAN DANTE, AUTHOR OF FLAME IN THE NIGHT

"Steeped in a heady, addictive mixture of possessive attraction and macabre eroticism, *A Thing Divine* is a lavish treat for connoisseurs of pitch-black, gothic romance where vampires are still true, dangerous monsters...and yet all the more alluring."

— CYRAN FARINGRAY, AUTHOR OF
LOVE LIKE GILDED BONES AND THE
HOUSE OF GRIEF

A Thing Divine

A Thing Divine

RIAN ADARA

BLACK
ROSE

A Thing Divine
written by Rian Adara
published by Black Rose,
an imprint of Quill & Crow Publishing House

Edited by Tiffany Putenis and Lisa Morris

Cover Design by Fay Lane

Interior by Cassandra L. Thompson

Printed in the United States of America

ISBN (ebook): 978-1-958228-64-7

ISBN (paperback): 978-1-958228-67-8

Publisher's Website: quillandcrowpublishinghouse.com

For those who don't mind darkness with their delights.

Publisher's Note

A Thing Divine is an erotic dark romance novel with horror elements that include graphic violence and gore. Please be sure to check the Trigger Index located in the back of the book for any potential triggers.

Chapter One

EHVY

"If of life you keep a care, shake off slumber, and beware..."

Everyone wants to see where the bodies are buried. The tour group ignores the angry gray clouds hovering overhead as they make their way to the crypt. Rumbling in the distance draws Ehvy's eyes skyward. It won't be long before the rain starts, yet no one seems bothered as they follow the docent with rapt attention. Ehvy hangs back, allowing the group to move ahead of her as she absorbs the rich green surroundings. A stark departure from the cement kingdom of London.

"While Sandridge descendants manage Highcombe Nigh, the family has long dispersed from the village, favoring locales that don't bear the history of the estate or their name," the docent says, his voice traveling over their heads. "Salacious parties, screams in the night, and villagers going missing haunt the history of Highcombe. It's why the family stopped using the crypt hundreds of years ago. A regular target for vandals over the centuries, people didn't allow the deceased Sandridges a moment's peace. America was still a colony the last time a Sandridge buried their kin here."

Lily, one of Ehvy's friends, peers over her shoulder and winks. "See? I told you this would be up your alley. A little something for all of us, yeah?"

"This'll give me nightmares," Gemma says as she leans closer to Lily. She glances over her shoulder at Ehvy, and even though her look is sharp, the woman's small smile is light. "It matches Ehvy's career perfectly."

"Except my career doesn't keep me up at night," Ehvy says as she tries to subdue her wild curls in the gusting winds.

Her career as a medical examiner. Where her friends are all lawyers or executives or other corner office roles, Ehvy lives in the city morgue's basement, prying secrets from dead flesh. She speaks for them when they can no longer speak for themselves.

The sky grumbles louder and Ehvy glances at the darkening clouds again. A couple of heads do the same, but a voice brings everyone's focus back to earth.

"Are any of the rumors true?" someone asks with a distinctly American accent, their jeans, chunky sneakers, and baseball cap speaking to the distinct style indicative of those from across the pond. "What did people think was going on here?"

The docent smirks as he places a palm against the stone door of the crypt. "Those buried here have taken their secrets to the grave. But what we know through stories passed across hearths and through homes is the tale of the mad earl who was found raving in the streets before sinking his teeth into the neck of an unfortunate soul who tried to help him." The docent leans forward, his eyes wide, and says, "That is where the stories start, not end." He smiles as the sky cracks.

The group gasps, and Ehvy flinches as a drop hits her cheek. Wind rushes her, wrapping her hair around her head, and she gives up trying to control it. A sharp chill slithers around her bare wrists, pulsing cold into her veins, and she pulls her jacket tighter.

A bright flash of light illuminates the sky just before thunder rips through the crowd. Another round of shrieks hit her ears as water drops pelt Ehvy's cheeks. People rummage for umbrellas and stowed jackets before the rain comes down in sheets.

"Let's make our way back inside so we don't get lashed. The tour's far from over!" The docent's chipper voice is a stark contrast to the rumbling clouds pressing in around the group as people skitter across the grass.

Ehvy's friends hurry up the knoll to the main entrance, heels, skirts, and white pants not compatible with the coming rainstorm. The crypt draws her attention, stone that appears damp with thick moss growing across one side of it. The green matches the grass as if the grounds are slowly consuming what's inside. Digesting the secrets of the Sandridge dead.

Highcombe Nigh looks like every other manor dotted across the English countryside she and her friends have visited. With busy lives come busy schedules, and their monthly outings aren't just an escape from the London grit but a getaway from daily tasks and expectations. Being child-free and single, there isn't much Ehvy needs to escape from, especially when she can cater to her hobbies and interests whenever the mood strikes. It's why she doesn't complain when they want to visit the country estates of the wealthy for the sake of fantasy. She appreciates these trips even more when her friends recognize where she's coming from and make it a point to include something more to her tastes, like Highcombe and its ghastly history.

She's long stopped trying to correct them when they try to talk about her "gothic" lifestyle. There's no one around who would look at her wild brown curls, cream-colored sweater, and suede riding boots and call Ehvy goth. She cuts them off at the knees when they try to insinuate that her career is what's keeping a partner away. If someone is too delicate to handle her career as a medical examiner, then they're not worthy of being with her. Ehvy would rather be thirty-six and single than saddled with an unfulfilling relationship.

The tour group falls into a queue, snaking its way up the extensive front stairs of the opulent manor. Her friends call her name, and she waves at them as she stares at the home, now a museum moonlighting as a sideshow for those interested in the shadows of English history. Lord knows there are plenty of them.

On a sunny day, the structure is surely striking, welcoming, and perhaps even dreamy, lending to the fantasies of her friends. Ehvy's seen enough in such light that she can buy the ideal. But now, as the rain turns steady, the manor is a monolith, looming and overbearing. Light struggles to penetrate the windows. The darkness inside absorbs any warmth.

Ehvy shivers as she approaches the heavy wooden doors yawning wide in front of her.

Velvet-upholstered chairs cluster in the corner, their cushions lush yet stiff. Ehvy imagines if she were to sit on one, she'd bounce right off. A couple nearby tuck their outdoor gear into bags as Ehvy moves deeper inside. Grand staircases sit on either side of the foyer. Dark, rich wood gleams in the light cast from the chandelier, and a blood-red runner hugs the stairs while a red velvet rope keeps tourists at bay.

Recklessness twitches Ehvy's muscles as she stares at the forbidden space, shadows hanging thick like curtains blocking her view. Something pricks at her mind, a flash of déjà vu. Walking up those stairs, the smooth, cold wood sliding under her fingers. Laughter bubbling in her throat.

The image—the *feeling*—is gone in a flash as the marble floor of the foyer echoes with voices, words blending together in a susurration of indecipherable noise. Ehvy's heart hammers as she blinks the manor back into focus and swallows hard. She's not sure what would make her think something like that. Perhaps Highcombe reminds her of something. Some manor she saw on TV, maybe. She doesn't know what else could have caused that feeling. Ehvy's never been here before.

A crack of lightning illuminates the foyer, turning the stained glass windows into an inferno of reds and yellows before the boom of thunder rattles the walls. A couple of shrieks resonate in the entryway, followed by nervous chuckles as the tour group gathers themselves.

As if the bolt split the sky, rain pours down in a torrent, soaking stone stairs and buses as a couple of people run indoors for safety. Ehvy's still close enough to the open door that a gust sprays her with mist before a couple of caretakers emerge from roped-off corridors to close it. A tinny rush of rain on the roof fills the cavernous space, the noise drumming uneasily into Ehvy's skin. As if she's afraid the roof itself will come crashing in.

The suggestion of a laugh tickles Ehvy's ear, a noise she might hear in the liminal space between awake and asleep. A noise she's not sure exists in or out of her head. The hum of the group still clamors through the foyer; the delicate laugh sounds again as if someone is standing over her shoulder. Ehvy looks behind her, but there's no one—nothing except a closed door. Sneakers squeak and heels clack against the marble as the docent directs the group down a corridor and away from her.

Shadows curl out from corners and reach for Ehvy as the light seems to follow the group. She doesn't realize the warmth they provide until their absence allows the chill of the manor to settle across her skin. The laugh sounds again, closer this time and louder, as the murmur of the group fades. Stronger. Bordering on a cackle. This time right at her ear, as if lips brush her skin.

The closest person is the teenager in the ticket booth with the blue glow of a cell phone on their face. Rattled, Ehvy clears her throat and walks the rest of the way across the foyer to catch up to the tail end of the group. Her boot taps become quiet when she hits the worn runner in the corridor, dozens of feet stomping it into the ground as the group huddles around a painting. It's lit with a mix of expertly placed candles and modern lights, creating a soft glow around a painted woman who looks sculpted from moonlight itself.

A pale, willowy creature graces the canvas, looking alive under the oils. Dressed in something Edwardian that accentuates a small breast and an even smaller waist, it's made of lush burgundy and lace while her pale blonde hair sits in curls upon her head. The look on her face speaks of something secretive, her smile like the Mona Lisa, but with more sass. Eyes a midnight black stare at Ehvy, piercing her as the fathomless gaze of the painted woman readies to swallow her whole.

Everyone always says that the eyes are the gateway to the soul, and Ehvy wonders if the painter posed her this way intentionally. It's just another painting of a noblewoman created with oils and brushes. Yet her eyes speak of something dark, something hiding behind the canvas that one must look close enough to see. Ehvy seems to be the only one seeing it, as the rest of the group watches the docent as he speaks.

The painting nags at her as she stares at it. Ehvy has seen that face before, but she knows *seen* isn't the right word. Experienced, maybe? It's a feeling she can't quite articulate, and it burrows deeper, nagging her to annoyance. Until the docent's words barge through.

"Rebecca Sandridge was the mistress of Highcombe at the turn of the twentieth century," the docent says as his eyes scan the crowd of eager tourists. "And a target of village whispers. She threw parties people would kill to get invited to, lasting well into the night." The wily man's eyebrow arches, and Ehvy can't help but arch hers back. The story feels like a tacky addition to the tour, but judging by the wide eyes and eager curls of nearby lips, the crowd devours it. "She and her husband, William Sandridge, had rather...curious sexual appetites. Deviance doesn't even begin to explain their tastes." The urge to roll her eyes is strong, but Ehvy refrains, instead crossing her arms over her chest and settling into her hips. "Unfortunately, the mistress met a tragic end in a carriage accident and at such a young age. Hardly thirty."

Lie.

The word is so intrusive, so sudden, Ehvy has to stifle a gasp with a subtle cough. The word spells itself out in her head as she feels it floating in her gut. She wracks her brain even harder to figure out where she's seen this woman before. It's on the tip of her tongue, so close yet out of reach, and Ehvy grunts in frustration.

Not until the group moves on to the next macabre attraction does it hit her: she knows Rebecca Sandridge from her dreams.

Except she doesn't think she's seen Rebecca's face. *She* was always the woman. Lithe and angular, long arms and legs that wrap around a man ready and willing to fall into them. Images flicker through her mind—hair that glows, even in the dark; a sultry smile like a spider weaving a web for its prey; and a man whose hands she could feel even in her dreams.

The impression of a figure climbing the stairs in the Highcombe foyer. The breath of a laugh.

Heat flushes Ehvy's cheeks as the memories of her dreams grow more detailed. They've been reoccurring for as long as she can remember, but it wasn't until she'd graduated from the university and started her career that they became...

salacious. Now is not the time to reminisce about *those* dreams.

A thump behind her draws her attention away from the migrating group, only for Ehvy to notice an empty corridor and foyer. Beyond that is another corridor blocked by yet another velvet rope. "No admittance," the rope insinuates, much like the one blocking the stairs from wandering tourists.

Normally, Ehvy would brush it off and rejoin the group. Farther down the corridor, they're already enthralled with something new. The docent motions with his hands as he speaks, but the words are lost in the growing distance between Ehvy and the group.

Another laugh, deep in her ear as an icy touch trails down her spine, sends decadent shivers across her body. The portrait of Rebecca stares at her, the knowing smile and penetrating gaze hypnotizing her. A word fills her mind, carving itself into her brain as it sluices through her veins.

Go.

With one more look over her shoulder, Ehvy notes the backs of her friends' heads as they stare, transfixed at whatever the docent is showing them. The historical rag that is Highcombe Nigh, polished to a high shine that begs respectability but is undercut by its sordid past, has bewitched even her friends.

She peeks into the foyer, expecting more tour groups, but it's empty. Blue light paints the ticket taker's face as they remain oblivious to her presence. Rumbling thunder vibrates through the manor, echoing into the soles of her boots as she walks quietly across the foyer and to the forbidden corridor. The light from the chandelier seems sharper, the muted gray sky from earlier faded into a black night, dulling the stained glass.

The rope keeping her out hooks into loops set in a carved wood frame and sits at about thigh height. With one more look at the ticket taker, Ehvy steps over the rope, then waits for someone to come after her. The docent and the group are gone, their voices little more than ghosts filtering through the massive home. No one stops her, so she continues down the forbidden passage.

There are no windows here, and the doors are all closed save for one at the far end. Electric lights illuminate ancient sconces along the walls, casting a soft glow over the lush red carpet and dark oak walls. Daintily lit portraits hang between the doors, showcasing men and women in clothes likely as old as the manor. Large collars and cinched waists, men in wigs, and women with delicate smiles on their faces. Where the tour is must be newer, showcasing Sandridges more recent than the Enlightenment.

Ehvy sees the resemblances among the portraits, however stylized they are. There is blood on these walls, on display despite the dark secrets they hold. Blood of the family that ran from this estate and manages it only when they must.

Candles drip wax onto candelabras along the walls or placed on tabletops. Whispers of heat from the flames graze her chilled skin as she walks. Ehvy gets closer to the lone open door where soft light beckons her inside, promising cozy comforts while setting her teeth on edge. Something rustles beyond her line of sight, and it's clear there is someone inside.

She shouldn't be here.

She turns to leave, abandoning her moment of rebellion.

Before she can walk away, a whiff of something catches her nose. A scented candle, perhaps. Sweet and delectable, calling her into the room. There and gone in an instant, Ehvy stops and wonders if she smelled anything at all. She takes a step closer to the forbidden room. More papers rustle, and someone sighs. A cackle rings through her ears, and the delicious scent hits her nose again before fading away like a ghost.

Against her better judgment, Ehvy allows the room to pull her closer until she walks across the threshold. Golden browns surround her. Old wood and the smell of musty books laced with something that makes her mouth water before it's gone again.

What the bloody hell is that smell?

Darkness draws her eye to a space on the far side of the room. A doorway. The cackle rings in her head again, and something like a fingernail trails itself across the back of her neck. Ehvy bites back the impression this manor is making on her as she keeps her eye on the dark doorway. The whispering in her ear demands she go to that darkness. Find out what it is. Her morbid curiosity says the same.

Meanwhile, her head—her logical brain—screams at her to go back.

"The public is not allowed back here. You should return to the tour."

The deep, authoritative voice jolts through her, the intrusion on her thoughts sending her heart pattering. She presses her hand to her chest and gasps, letting the realization that she's not alone settle over her after the initial shock of the man's voice. She knew there was probably someone in here, but that smell wiped away all reason.

It's a demanding voice, yet it sounds bored, weary. Exhausted. Something strums inside of her, and she turns away from the darkened room and notices the details of the space around her, and the man in it, for the first time. The sound of his voice says more than the words themselves, striking a chord deep within her she didn't know could be plucked. Something familiar. Like the portrait of Rebecca Sandridge, the manor itself, as though Ehvy's heard his voice in her dreams.

A large oak desk centers the built-in bookshelves behind it. Papers lay scattered across the tabletop, and an open laptop weighs them down. A hand shadowed by flickering candlelight glides a pen across the paper while the other well-manicured one rests on top of yet more papers.

The soft light of the room casts long shadows over the man's head, but she can tell his hair is dirty blonde and long enough to hang around his ears. He hasn't looked up from his work, and she suspects he isn't going to. She looks back at the darkened door, the mystery behind it still calling to her, but the man's unwelcoming tone stops her in her tracks. Whatever was pulling her here has disappeared. Now everything in her screams to run. Danger. Get away. Except for a little voice—something deeper, primal—telling her to stay right where she is.

"I'm sorry," Ehvy says breathlessly, her heart not calmed yet.

She should stop there and walk out of the room, leaving the man to whatever it is he's working on. Unfortunately, her mouth has a mind of its own, and the words flow before she can stop them.

"I'm sorry," Ehvy says again as heat floods her cheeks.

"This just seemed more exciting than the tour, and I, uh, thought I smelled something good, like a candle, so I followed my nose." A nervous chuckle escapes her lips, and her body heats to a temperature more like the surface of the sun. "It's stupid, I know."

His head slowly rises, eyes dragging from his work and up her body until his gaze rests on her face. His look is hard and unmoving, his brow furrowed, lips pursed. Until something shifts, something like shock flickering through his eyes before it's gone, leaving Ehvy with a man staring at her as if he's just found something he's been looking for.

Soft, pink lips part as he stares at her. An aquiline nose sits between dark eyes; Ehvy can't tell if they are actually dark or if the room is casting shadows on him. Pale cheeks cave the slightest hint, giving him an angular look that makes her want to trace her finger along the hard lines of his face. He's the most beautiful man she's ever seen...and so familiar.

The man who opens his arms to her in her dreams. The dreams when she's Rebecca.

Jesus, is this the man she's been seeing in her dreams for years? No. It can't be. The literal man of her dreams?

Fuck off. Impossible. That's ridiculous.

Things like this only happen in fiction and not to thornbacks with a career dissecting corpses. Yet...

Time grinds to a halt. Then, as if something kicks in her head, she realizes she's been staring. He's been staring, too, the age of centuries in his eyes as they watch her. She must go. Save herself further embarrassment. Her head screams *yes, finally, go now,* but that swirling primal urge building inside her is a devil, whispering in her ear that she should stay.

Awkward laughter erupts from Ehvy's mouth, and if she flushes anymore, she will combust. "I'll just go. Sorry again for barging in."

Before her head could burst into flames and the man could throw her out by her ear, she spins and scurries for the door. Ehvy pulls her jacket tighter around her shoulders and ducks her head, trying to make herself smaller in his presence. Trying to shut out the voice inside her—the feeling inside of her—telling her she is exactly where she's meant to be.

"Wait."

The word is like a hand on her shoulder, begging her not to move. The tenor of his voice pierces her booted feet to the floor. It's a demand and a plea, and she thrills with the notes of it.

She looks over her shoulder and watches him stand. The first couple buttons of his shirt are open, exposing a triangle of chest that draws her eye. Sleeves sit folded at mid-arm, exposing a silver watch on his left wrist. His ring finger is noticeably empty, and Ehvy swallows hard. Tailored black pants sit on narrow hips, held in place by a belt with a delicate buckle. He drags his fingers across the desktop while tucking the other hand in a pocket.

Run. Go. Ehvy's rational brain screams while something else says *stay.* Something not her, yet rooted in her soul.

A heady mix of seduction and death pulses off him as if he's just walked out of a crypt, ready to kill the first bright thing he sees. Ehvy has no idea where these thoughts come from. It's as if she's reading him, seeing into the soul he drags behind him while it kicks and screams to get away. He is poison, and her instincts scream to escape. Yet she knows poison can be oh-so-sweet.

He walks around the corner of the desk slowly, his steps deliberate yet making no sound as he treads across the worn carpet. Once at the edge of the desk, he settles against it and places his other hand in his pocket while staring at her, a tilt to his head. A predator admiring his prey.

"What smell?"

Chapter Two

WILL

"...she is mortal; but by immortal Providence she's mine..."

Blood.

She smells the blood.

Impossible.

Yet there's no tantalizing scented candle in his study. Surely, chandlers today don't make blood-scented candles. However, this delicious thing in front of him says she "smelled something good." There is nothing *good* in this room—or the next—that she could smell, let alone something that smells good to the likes of her. To Will, even after nearly a thousand years, blood is the most delicious scent. It's the smell of roasting meat or baked goods to a human, but this morsel before him says something smells good.

How very interesting.

Pink tinges her cheeks, and her eyes flutter as she

searches for the right thing to say. Fingers knot in front of her, knuckles blanching white like bone. Her eyes dart toward the door, her fingers continuing to twist as if she hears something. Nobody else is around. Only the two of them. She turns her head back around. Her tongue darts over her lips, and she clears her throat.

She points to a nearby candle, the flame flickering in an unfelt breeze. "One of the tapers, maybe? I'm not sure," she says with an awkward smile.

Something deep within Will pulses.

The more he looks at her, the more impossible this entire event seems. Blood flows under the woman's skin, and her heart flutters under her breasts. The familiarity of her overwhelms him, yet he knows he's never met her before. The expressions that cross her face aren't familiar.

All the while, something deep within him screams for her, a yearning that knocks him to his knees. Something he hasn't felt in a hundred years. Something he never expected to feel again. There's only one person who has stirred up such feelings in him. One other person who allowed the scent of blood to draw her to him.

Rebecca.

His love has been dead for almost a century, swept out like a rug from under him. A fortuitous error in their protections and the villagers took advantage. They made sure Rebecca could not save herself, and Will wasn't fast enough to stop them. He's lived with that guilt ever since, the sting of it lessening by degrees over the years.

Now, here she stands, in the same place he met Rebecca all those centuries ago. They are the opposite in so many ways, yet this sweet thing before him throbs with the same desires Rebecca did. Her soul sings to him in the same way. Her nose drew her to him much the way Rebecca's did.

His Rebecca was the only person who not only stomached his desires but partook. Vampirism takes its toll on many, but not him. Or her. They were together five hundred years before things went awry.

Confusion swirls inside Will. Rebecca isn't reborn in this modern parcel of flesh. The witch would have never brought her back, and he had no clue if that was even possible. Over the course of his long life, reincarnation has never been more than a fantasy—a way for someone to see something that wasn't there. Will never believed in it, but as this woman continues to fidget before him, he questions everything he thought he knew.

Where Rebecca was nearly his height and lithe with pale blonde hair in wisps around her shoulders, this woman is shorter. Her head just scrapes his chin, skin golden, a mass of curly dark hair framing her face with the meat of the modern world on her bones. His gums ache with the desire to bite into her.

He laughs, a disarming sound, and runs his hands through his artfully disheveled hair. "The tour can be droll; you are not intruding."

There is nothing about this moment that is an intrusion.

She appears as enthralled with him as he is with her. Her eyes travel over his face, lingering at his neck before darting to the room behind him. As if on cue, a wheeze hisses from the adjoining room, hardly perceptible even to his heightened hearing, yet he worries this mortal woman may still hear. Lucky for him, the slab of meat hidden away behind him can't speak. One needs vocal cords to do that, and Will removed them himself.

Will shuffles, covering any hint of untoward sound she may hear and takes a step closer. "It must have been my dinner," Will says, allowing the corner of his mouth to curl into a small smile. "I just finished, and my chef is excellent."

"Your chef?" she says, her thick eyebrows rising as she lowers her hands.

Let me in, he thinks. *Open your arms to me.*

He must know more about her. Is this truly Rebecca, or is she something else?

Vampires have powers of persuasion, but he will not command her nor influence her decisions toward him, no matter how much his ancient heart screams for him to do it. She will come to him of her own free will. He will make sure of it.

Will looks at her from under his lashes, a sultry gaze he perfected over the centuries thanks to Rebecca's tutelage. *Charm*, she once said, *works just as well as any magic.*

He casts his gaze around the study. Ancient timber and swirling smoke from table-side candles thicken the air, anachronistic to the laptop and cell phone on his desk.

"This is my family's home; the chef is on my payroll."

Tension releases from her shoulders and her knees soften.

Good.

Her eyes narrow in good humor as a smile flirts with her luscious lips. "Am I supposed to believe that?"

Disbelief flickers in her gaze. That she's speaking to him in such a way, perhaps. Or that he's returning the enticement, or perhaps that he hasn't thrown her out yet, some pleb dragging dirt-caked shoes through his home.

There is nothing plebeian about this woman.

"What else is there to believe?" He levels his gaze on her.

The unbelievable, if her nose is anything to go by. The blood she can't possibly smell yet appears to smell all the same. His ancient heart thunders in his chest the more he considers it. To believe in reincarnation is to believe that vampires possess souls. That there would be another just like Rebecca to enter his life is even more unlikely. There was only one. It would explain why this creature is unremarkable at first glance. Anything but upon a second look.

"Ehvy!" someone yells down the cavernous corridor, and she whips her head to the open door for a second time. "Where'd you go?"

Ehvy. Her name.

When she looks back at him, her face is regretful. "I'm sorry, I'll leave you alone. I apologize for intruding."

She takes the meek stance of most women today, apologizing too much for her existence despite his eagerness for her life. He will fix this.

"Please," he says as she steps toward the door, readying to leave him. He can't let her get away. Not yet. Not until he has answers about who Ehvy is. "I apologize for the lackluster tour. I can give you a far more intriguing one than what you paid for. The fee is simply your company."

It feels like a line as soon as it leaves his mouth, some sleazy hook to give the beauty before him an "intriguing tour" of his home. But as the corners of her mouth flutter into a hint of a smile, he knows she is not dissuaded. His ask is genuine, and she senses it. He can feel it in the flutter of her heart and the quickening of her pulse.

Nerves threaten her acquiescence, though. The muscles in her shapely legs shake imperceptibly, her mind surely telling her to run rather than take him up on his offer. He knows she could very well never come back. But the intoxicating scent in the air and the magnetic pull between them muddles reason and common sense. So much so he can feel her considering it. She just needs one final push.

"I'm Will," he says as he steps forward, his hand out.

Ehvy glances at it, then closes the gap between them, her hand reaching for his. Skin slides across skin as their fingers grip each other.

"Thursday. If you are free, come back around at half-six."

She hesitates, still mulling over the offer. She wants this, but the modern word has drilled alertness and skepticism into her psyche.

"Staff is always present on the grounds. We will not be alone in the house. Allow me to give you my number and if you decide to use it, then I will have yours."

The assurances he gives are few and thin, and judging by the way her eyes light, she knows it as well. If only he could read her mind; it was a skill few vampires possess. But he can read her body. Desire throbs between her legs with her need for him, dampening that apex he desperately wants to tear apart. The smell of her lust entices him the same way the blood entices her. The war of her decision scrawls across her face. Will doesn't need to be a vampire to see that.

When the silence grows heavy, she finally says, "I think I can make that." She pulls her cell phone from her bag and turns her luscious brown eyes on him, so unlike Rebecca's deep blue. "Your surname?"

Will presses his tongue to his canine as he smiles. "Sandridge."

Ehvy smirks, the reluctant look in her eyes telling him what her voice doesn't — she doesn't believe him. If he were her, he wouldn't believe him either. Likely, she will do what most women today do before experimenting further with a potential partner: research. The internet is such a marvelous thing.

"Perhaps I will see you on Thursday," Ehvy says, a coquettish look that speaks volumes more than what she likely intends.

It's a look Rebecca used to wear when hunting. Will's knees go weak, but he holds himself steady. He wishes Ehvy would turn that look on him again just so he can see it one more time before she goes.

The grating soprano calls down the corridor again. It takes the strength of ages to keep a sneer from crawling across his face at the sound. If it wouldn't frighten her away, he would snuff out the intrusion in a heartbeat. She lingers for a moment longer, longing in her eyes that he hopes he reflects in his before she concedes to the annoyance calling her name and exits his life.

For now.

She walks out with a muted smile. Her round face and sun-kissed skin bewitched him in a way he hadn't experienced in ages. He can't help but feel some pathetic romantic notion of yearning and desire. It overwhelms and somewhat annoys him, this silly human emotion for the lovesick. Perhaps it's because his life has been void of such feelings for so long. He's out of practice. It's been decades since he's looked at anyone, especially a human, with anything other than bloodlust.

He hardly remembers what Rebecca was like as a human. The day she walked into the manor is little more than a hazy dream now. By then, the rumors were endemic and inescapable. Finding help to tend his home was thin on the best of days. Rebecca was a maid; her mother had just died, and her father had gone long before that. She was beautiful, even in the drab clothes of the help.

Will often caught her staring, and he couldn't help but return the look. They exchanged little more than pleasantries, skirting around each other like the masters and the help are wont to do. Until Rebecca wandered where she shouldn't have—one of the dungeon rooms that was occupied with Will's dinner.

She gasped, shocked at the sight, but intrigue quickly took over. Rebecca didn't shy away from the victim, their abdomen torn open and organs spilling onto the stone floor. She stepped closer, her hand out, fingers grazing along the exposed intestines. When Will stepped out of the shadows to confront her, she didn't cower. Instead, she moved closer to him, her gaze inquisitive. Yearning. She wiped a bit of blood onto her lips, and he was lost from that moment on.

Will sighs, his palm tingling with her touch. The scent of Ehvy lingers in the air, mixing with the heady scent of blood from the other room and the memory of Rebecca floating through his mind. He'll need to see the witch and find out what the bloody hell is going on. Ehvy's very essence is Rebecca, if not her body. This should not be...yet it is. The witch will have answers, even if he has to peel them out of her.

His cock throbs, and he pulls at his pants as he stares at the space Ehvy just occupied. His dinner wheezes again, and he sighs before turning and taking long strides into the dark room. A flayed body thrown over the desk greets him, the chest cavity cracked open and waiting. Blood permeates the air, and Will's gums pulse. It's the scent Ehvy followed. What drew her to him.

Bloody eyelids flutter, the exposed lungs expanding and contracting in shallow breaths. The only signs the mangled thing is still alive. Will runs a finger along a blood-coated rib before sticking it in his mouth, savoring the flavor and wondering if Ehvy tastes like Rebecca or if she will have her own sweet flavor.

His cock pulses painfully, and he unbuckles his belt, unzipping his pants and pulling himself free, his member solid and in need of release. He plunges his fist through blood-covered ribs, bones snapping under his force, and wraps his hand around the barely beating heart. His free hand grabs his length and moves in slow, tortuous strokes. The body gasps, labored breaths growing faster as the heart pounds in his hand.

Will closes his eyes, remembering how he and Rebecca fucked on a bed covered in the viscera of their dinner, the feel of her flesh, the taste of her dipped in blood. How she shoved her fingers in his mouth as she rode him, tasting of life. Blood called to Rebecca the same way it called to Ehvy. Will wonders if she will embrace him the way Rebecca had —without judgment and with gusto.

The memory of Rebecca morphs into a fantasy of Ehvy.

Her hands on him, her pussy clamped around his cock instead of his hand. Blood drips down her chest, and Will laps it up, sinking his fangs into a supple, tender breast as she writhes on top of him.

Will she want him the way he wants her? The way Rebecca wanted him? Yes. It was in her eyes as her gaze raked over him. He felt it in her touch as it lingered on him. The need pulsed off of her like the heady scent of roses in bloom. She may just need some convincing to throw off the shackles of society.

The pleasure builds in the pit of his stomach, his cock growing harder as his strokes move faster. Eager pants clog his throat, his body going rigid as ecstasy crashes into him. He spills himself across the carnage, his fist clenching onto the heart as it pulses its last beat before he rips it out. His ears ring as he lightly strokes his sensitive dick, thoughts of Ehvy running through his head.

He marvels at the heart in his hand. The weight of it, the density, before sinking his teeth into the muscle. Blood squirts across his tongue, and his eyes roll into the back of his head, seeing nothing but Ehvy.

Chapter Three

EHVY

"You have often begun to tell me what I am, but stopped and left me to a bootless inquisition."

Never in her wildest dreams, pun intended, did Ehvy think she was dreaming about real people. Sure, there's the woo-woo notion that dreams can link to past lives. Then there's the other idea—that they are nothing more than a parade of things one has seen over the course of a lifetime. Each face, each place, cataloged in the brain and pulled out of a hat at random when one sleeps. The only logical answer that she has for both Rebecca *and* Will showing up in her dreams is coincidence. She *had* to have seen both of them before. In an old book, maybe. Or on some website she looked at before going to Highcombe Nigh.

Still, the knowledge nags at her, tap dancing across her mind as she tries to enjoy brunch with her friends. A shorter trip than the tours they take, one she usually enjoys without distraction, but her mind won't let her focus on the conversation.

Highcombe. Will. Rebecca's portrait. It's going to nag her if she doesn't figure it out.

Her friends try to get more information out of her, especially Lily since she was the one who went looking for her, but Ehvy brushes them off. Instead of telling them about the handsome man she met in a forbidden study, she tells them a random painting caught her eye, and she wandered off. She doesn't quite know what possesses her to keep Will to herself, but it's as if lips press to the shell of her ear and whisper *hush*.

As they're wrapping up, Ehvy, two mimosas deep and a flush to her body, bids goodbye to her friends. Under normal circumstances, she'd head back to her flat in West Brompton for a lazy Sunday before the dead call her back to work on Monday morning. Today, her destination is The British Library near King's Cross.

One thing London has is historical knowledge. Thousands of years old and with conservation out the ears, it's easy to find just about anything on—well, anything. Highcombe Nigh and the alleged owner itself being no exception. The few Google searches Ehvy tried the night before didn't turn up much, not with a generic name like William Sandridge. Tying it to Highcombe Nigh and Iverham—the small village where Highcombe sits—nets little more. So it's to the library she goes to find information that might not have made the digital transformation.

She spends hours digging through archives, following every crumb she can find on Highcombe Nigh and the

Sandridges. All she has to go on is information from the docent and the general tourist information from the website. There are more legends than facts, and it drives Ehvy up a wall. She doesn't want ghost stories. She wants to make sure she's not walking into a night alone with a serial killer.

There are scattered reports of missing people around Iverham over the centuries, but nothing that sets the hairs on the back of her neck standing. Whatever stories the docent was prattling on about seem to be just that—stories.

Gossip columns from the turn of the twentieth century, for what those are worth, mention parties lasting all hours and lights blazing from the windows until dawn. No one saw anyone coming or going from the manor. Music often traveled into the valley, little more than whispers on the wind, yet the villagers heard it. The nearby gentry would seethe in jealousy, affronted at their exclusion from whatever affairs their neighbors were having, and let the papers know their displeasure. If nothing else, it was amusing to read and somewhat validated the ridiculous stories the docent spun.

The Sandridges appeared to stay mum about it all. There was never any response from the manor's residents or staff in the paper. The village whispers never seemed to bother them. What ruffled the most feathers was the Sandridge family's self-exclusion from society. Not much of a scandal, especially nowadays.

Ehvy blows a curl out of her face and falls back into the chair with a grunt, eliciting a terse stare from someone nearby. She grinds her teeth, grabs a nearby paper, yellowed with age, and gently turns the pages. Her eyes skim the microscopic words until a marriage announcement snags her attention.

Sandridge. William and Rebecca.

The photo makes her jolt upright, an audible gasp echoing around the quiet worktable. Someone shushes her from nearby, but she pays them no mind. Instead, she flips to the front of the paper and checks the date: 1906. Paper rustles as she turns back to the announcement and the photo that freezes her to the spot.

Staring back at her are two faces she knows she can place.

The woman, Rebecca, is the same one from the portrait at Highcombe. She's wearing a similar style dress, her already lithe waist cinched, hair arranged in an updo stuck with glittering combs. The woman in this photo carries that same presence as the portrait. From Ehvy's very dream. A face she'd never seen, yet she knows it intimately, like it at one point belonged to her.

Rebecca's eyes track Ehvy's movements from the yellowed photo. Her gaze is just as penetrating as her portrait's. Ehvy's nerves rattle as she leans away from the table and watches Rebecca's eyes move with her. A breath of a laugh tickles Ehvy's ear, and she brushes it away with her shoulder, her heart growing louder the more she stares at the photo, and it stares back.

The man in this photo is the same man she saw in the Highcombe study yesterday. High cheekbones, penetrating gaze, tall, lean frame hidden under a suit slightly larger than fitting, indicative of the style of the day. The man in this hundred-plus-year-old photo might as well be Will.

Both of them are unsmiling as they stand next to each other. William's arm drapes around Rebecca's back while both of her hands hold one of his in front. William stares into the camera as if impatient, eager to get on with his new wife.

Ehvy's rational brain stutters. Of course, they're not the same person. More than a hundred years separate the man in the photo and the Will she met at Highcombe yesterday. There has to be another explanation.

King George V and Czar Nikolai were spitting images of each other. There are any number of genetic circumstances that could have an ancestor to today's Will look just like the historical version. And it's not like a name like William Sandridge is unique. But Rebecca and Highcombe, the portrait hanging on the wall of Will's home. That's a harder sell. The photograph is impossible to look away from.

While Highcombe's history appears to be mundane, despite what the paid tour says, a swirl of something unsettled spins in Ehvy's stomach. As if she's missing something.

She frowns and places her hand on the mouse, fingers slick with anxious sweat as she wakes up the computer in front of her. She tinkers with her previous search terms, pulling keywords from articles that might narrow things down for her about who Will Sandridge—the one she met yesterday—actually is.

Several limited liability companies pop up, along with some incorporated businesses. Someone of his wealth would have things like real estate holdings, shell accounts for various things, whatever rich people like him have. Unfortunately, the search doesn't give her much substantial information, and Ehvy's not an investigative journalist. Short of snooping in his desk drawers, she doesn't know where else to look. Pulling up the names of a few holding companies gives her little more than crumbs. Just enough to tell her he's likely who he says he is, if the photo of his ancestor didn't already confirm that.

Assuming that is his ancestor.

She can't stop the thought from crawling through her head. A smile flirts with her lips as she chuckles—the notion is ridiculous. There is no explanation that would support the Will of today and the William of a century ago being the same person.

No *rational* explanation.

No real world explanation, and Ehvy lives in the real world.

Tired of the dead ends she keeps hitting looking into Will, she tries probing into the history of Highcombe Nigh itself. The current manor is almost five hundred years old and stands in place of a much older structure that was torn down to make room for the newer one. There are some pictures of wood reliefs and lithographs of what stood there before, something far more castle-like.

Tying it back to the Sandridges, and Will specifically, tells her it was Night Castle before the family tore it down. Sat on top of a large hill, the windows were hardly ever lit; it often blended into the night sky, hence its name. But it's the story attached to the very beginnings of the castle that gets the hairs on the back of her neck to stand on end.

Tucked away on a link from a link from a link, on a site with garish fonts and old wood reliefs of suspect origin, Ehvy reads about the original earl of the castle, a man named Charles who disappeared one evening. None of the servants could find him, and his children and wife came up empty-handed. Until someone found him wandering the village with his clothes torn and blood dripping from his mouth.

As if that wasn't bad enough, he attacked people when they came near. Snarling, trying to bite their necks. On one person, he did succeed, tearing the vein from their throat as he knelt over his victim, draining them of blood.

Help from the castle arrived and carted him off. Money fixes all things, and these problems disappeared as though they'd never happened. The villagers never saw him again. They never saw his wife or children again either, and the windows stayed dark.

Guests who were unfortunate enough to enter the castle never returned, which fed the fires of rumor for centuries. It wasn't until the family built a new structure that the whispers of the castle's history finally died. As though the new manor could frighten away the ghosts of the past.

The docent barely touched on these details during the tour, probably because they sounded like unsubstantiated rubbish. Spooky rumors meant to entice tourists on the official tour are one thing. Actual accusations of the supernatural? That's a bit much.

Because what these stories point to, especially that of the first earl of Sandridge, is vampires. Fictional creatures of the night that don't exist in the real world. They're scary stories children tell each other or adults read to escape the technological hellscape the world has become.

The open encyclopedia on the table mocks her. Ehvy wants answers. Some clarity around Highcombe Nigh and Will. She clears her throat and sits up, the macabre images on the screen pulsing. The marriage photo in the nearby paper haunts her. Will's cloned face and Rebecca's stare pull her deeper into the mystery.

Her fingers whirl across the keyboard, trying one more

search to see if she can dig up anything on the mysterious Sandridges. This time, Rebecca. Except "Rebecca Sandridge" turns up little more than a marriage certificate in the archive catalog. The woman is as much of a ghost as she looks, existing in the deceased Sandridge's mind alone.

William's mind.

Will's mind?

No matter how much she tries to convince herself, Ehvy ties the historical William Sandridge to the modern one. It's impossible not to. She glances at the photo again and frowns as if her eyes are lying to her. The man in that photo looks just like Will. They could be identical twins. It is only natural that her mind wants to combine them into one.

With an aggravated sigh, Ehvy returns the materials and leaves. She found nothing bad about Will. No headlines she should be concerned with. No off-putting dating app profiles that would have her running. Her look into Will, at least as of right now, is neutral. It makes traveling back to Highcombe in the middle of the week a little less stressful.

The history of Highcombe and the Sandridges makes her skin itch, though. They should be nothing more than fanciful stories created by yellow journalism and people with too much time on their hands. It's easier to ascribe the shitty acts of man to something devilish than accepting they're bad people. Yet this doesn't quiet Ehvy's mind.

She pulls on a jacket, a smile creeping across her face at the thought of Will as some prince of darkness driven by nothing more than the need to bite into her neck and drink her blood until she dies. It's hilarious, and Ehvy keeps the smile on her face despite the tiny nagging thought poking at the back of her mind asking, *what if?* She's always liked a good bite, but blood's never been her kink. Yet she can't deny the swirl of pleasure it brings her to think about Will's bloodied face as she licks him clean.

For fuck's sake. What the hell is wrong with me?

As she steps out of the library, brakes squeal, and horns blare as steel crunches into steel. Arms and legs sail through the air before a body crashes into the windshield of a double-decker bus. They slide down the front end before thudding to the road in a bloody heap. Ehvy gasps at the scene as people rush around her. Car doors slam, the bus's doors open, and sirens flare to life in the distance. The knot of cars on the street stops all traffic as a crowd gathers.

Ehvy wonders if she should do something. She is a doctor, but her expertise isn't in keeping people alive. It's in death. No matter how much death she sees on a daily basis, life being ripped away is something else entirely.

Morbid curiosity draws her to the curb, close enough to see the blood streaked against the cracked windshield. Then the smell hits her like a slap, thick and cloying and sweet. Her mouth waters. The same smell from Will's study yesterday. No candles, he said. Maybe it was his meal.

A meal that smells like fresh blood?

She smells it as she peers through the throng of people, her mouth-watering even though her stomach turns. Shoulders part, and for just a moment, she sees the heap of mangled flesh and fresh blood that was a person, their crumpled bicycle under a car's tire nearby. It hits her as strong as standing in a kitchen over a stove with a sizzling steak.

That sultry scent from Will's study, what she smells now, is blood.

Impossible.

Ehvy's around blood all the time. She's regularly elbow-deep in bodies, and she's never had this kind of reaction before.

Dead blood isn't fresh.

The thought filters through the carnage in front of her, forcing Ehvy to choke down a cackle. No. It can't be. The nose and the brain can do strange things. She just spent all afternoon in the library digging into Will's past. His bloody family history featured an ancestor who went mad and tried to drink someone's blood. Her thoughts are all tied up. Nothing else.

She pushes her way through the crowd toward King's Cross. That's more than enough for one day. No one has ever turned her around like this before. Like she's some lovesick schoolgirl who lets a new boy occupy the entirety of her thoughts. Ridiculous is what it is.

Blood doesn't make her sick. Medical school and her current occupation killed that sensitivity years ago. As the Tube careens toward her stop, she wishes her stomach would roil—not at her reaction to the blood, but the carnage itself. She presses a hand to her gut, calling up images of the wreck like some morbid true crime junkie. Yet even thinking about the smell makes her mouth water.

It couldn't have been the blood. It's just not possible. She caught a whiff of a kebab shop nearby, maybe. There are any number of rational explanations that don't include Ehvy having a newfound desire to consume human blood.

Will's face flickers through her mind as she bobs along with the train car. The sharp planes of his face. His endearing smile. Something pulses deep in her core, and she sighs at the feeling, luxuriating in it and cursing herself for it.

Lovesick schoolgirl.

They've spent all of five minutes together, yet she can't get him out of her head. Hell, that she traveled across the city to look into him speaks volumes. No one else in her dating life has warranted this kind of effort. Yet here she is.

Then again, no one else in her dating life owned a country manor that would require additional effort to get to in the event of something untoward happening. Ehvy's only thinking of her own safety, of course. But that would also beg her to tell her friends where she's going come Thursday and she hasn't. There's no point in getting them involved so early in the game.

Never mind that Will is literally the man of her dreams, and she's convinced she's been Rebecca in those same dreams. The dreams that have been recurring her whole life, starring a couple that existed more than a hundred years ago.

It's just one big coincidence.

All of it. Will is just another man. An attractive man that Ehvy can't wait to see.

Lovesick fool.

Chapter Four

WILL

*"The mistress which I serve quickens what's dead
and makes my labors pleasures..."*

W ill wraps his fingers around the gearshift and
shoves it into third as he presses the accelerator.
The open window on his cream-colored Austin Healey 3000
allows in the chilled night air without it washing over him as
if the top were down. While he is mostly immune to the
cold, that much wind in his face annoys him. It's cool
enough with it up to keep the heated thoughts of Ehvy from
taking over his mind.

How entirely mortal and aggravating that such a thing
has him so turned around. Perhaps because it's been a
century since he's seen Rebecca, and emotion overwhelms
his mind. Ehvy's presence has triggered him. She looks
nothing like his lost love, yet she pulses with such similar life.

Her call to blood, and to him, further evidence that some version of Rebecca lies buried deep within her.

The engine revs around a sharp turn as he continues his drive to Littlewick. The witch must know he's coming by now. She's far too aware of these things for her own good, and it's nearly gotten her killed many times over the last four hundred years. It unnerves him how his moods leave the woman unfazed, yet he can't help but admire her for how she stands up to him. Few do, and even fewer live to speak of it. If she were still a cowering whelp after all this time, she'd be even more insufferable.

The witch's cottage is little more than a shed set in the middle of the countryside. A low stone wall surrounds the grounds, hand-placed hundreds of years ago, just before she entangled herself with the Sandridge estate. What surrounds her cottage aren't mere plants; protective herbs and spells line all of the entrances and even the soil itself.

Before him, she was a simple villager with eccentric healing capabilities. After they became reluctant partners, she unearthed magic that would normally draw fiery attention, but it has only protected her thanks in part to him. Not only has he allowed her magical practice to flourish in service to his needs, but he's also eliminated any whiffs of witch hunts pointed her way. Thoughts of the witch always aggravate him; he slams the gear shift into fourth as the engine roars. Unfortunately, his options are few. Her grudging help has gotten him this far. If nothing else, she's making herself useful.

The lane to her house is long and winding, gravel and stone popping under his tires as Will pulls up to the front door. A silhouette lingers in the lit window and he smirks, thinking about the frown pressing down on her face at the sight of him. She is never thrilled to see him and wants him gone faster than she can help him. He always said he'd linger just to piss her off, but more often than not, he grows weary of her too quickly for that.

The turn of the key in the ignition sends a resounding click throughout the car as the engine's purr quiets. His handcrafted chestnut Trickers shoes stand stark against the gritty lane when he steps out. Yet the grit eludes even the lowest hem of his Davies suit. He strikes a cutting figure against the homely abode of the witch. The difference is even more evident when she throws open the door and greets him with a scowl in her hand-dyed skirt and self-knit sweater.

"My world was better when you weren't in it," she hisses as a cat slinks out the door, paying Will no mind, its tail curled in a question mark.

Will smirks as he adjusts his blazer and steps toward the cottage, only to thump into an invisible barrier. The wards around her home keep him out until she grants him access. He rolls his eyes, sliding his hands into his pockets, and stares at the witch, not deigning to respond to her. Her complaining about him is irrelevant.

Their magical partnership does not prevent her from taking her own life. So, no matter how much she complains, she doesn't hate him enough to end herself. It would be an annoyance for him and require additional planning and care for his needs, but it would be far from unmanageable. He handles things well enough when he leaves the isle.

"If it means you will leave sooner, then come in," she says with a wave and shuffles back into her home.

Like pressure releasing, the invisible barrier disappears.

Will takes a breath and steps forward, treading firmly along the stone path. Thick wafts of wildflowers and herbs tickle his nose, though the scent of something much stronger pierces his senses and waters his eyes. That vile woman let the barrier down, but it does nothing for the protective fucking plants in her garden. Will sneers as he removes a hand from his pocket and pushes the door wider, allowing him better access to her home.

Inside, ancient furniture and moth-eaten throws cramp the cottage, and it smells faintly of cats. He does his best to keep his nose from wrinkling, but the musty smell is over-whelming. Unwashed bodies, mixed potent herbs, and boiled cheese. He would not put it past her to affix her premises purposely just to repel him more.

"I already give you what you want. Our deal doesn't extend beyond that."

Plates clatter as she speaks, and a kettle whistles before she moves it off the burner. He watches her work, her exterior dowdy and unkempt, but he knows better. The woman can move like a fox with the fatality of a lion. No genuine match for him, at least without her insipid magic, but she's not one to underestimate.

"I seek answers," Will tells her.

Common courtesy would require her to extend him an invitation for tea, but the witch is not common and she will extend no courtesy to him. What she gives him is spells and witchery that erase the bloody trails that would otherwise lead straight to him. Whispers of disappearances, fuel to the fire that is Highcombe Nigh, are kept to little more than embers through her efforts. When Will comes home every handful of decades, she makes sure his crimes go unnoticed.

She curses him for it with meaningless words. Any harm she attempts to afflict on him will come back to her. It was part of their deal. He was never going to allow her to obtain the upper hand and hold *his* life in *her* palm. Holding one of her children hostage until she complied made her all the more amenable to doing exactly what Will demanded. Killing him isn't an option, either. In the end, the witch was greedy. Eternal life that didn't require blood sustenance was too tempting for her to ignore, and Will capitalized on that. Rebecca, better versed in the magical arts than he, made sure it was a symbiotic relationship, one in which they both benefited from far more than the witch did. Threatening the other child helped solidify their pact the way Will needed.

"What answers could you possibly seek that you can't find yourself?" she says as she drops a sugar cube into her dainty cup.

Their unique situation is why she speaks to him the way she does. In this day and age especially, making someone disappear is harder than it used to be, and bona fide practicing witches are even harder to come by. She's too valuable of a resource. While Will could kill her in an instant, attempting to replace her wouldn't be worth the effort, and she knows it. Perhaps this is the witch's revenge. A slow needling of his patience over the centuries.

"What do you know of the dead coming back to life?" Will asks with an uptick of his brow.

She snorts into her teacup, splashing tea on the saucer. "Nigh on impossible. There are so few actual necromancers in this world, and their trade is difficult to hide. People would know if a reanimated corpse shambled down their street."

His first reaction is to shove his hand into her throat for her insubordination, but a millennium of control takes over and he forces a tight, humorless smile at her.

"I misspoke. I don't believe this woman has actually crawled out of her grave. Her essence, her soul, reminds me of someone." He rolls his hand in front of him, drawing the words from his mouth.

The witch's eyes narrow as she looks at him, her teacup to her lips. "You mean that dreadful woman? Between the two of you, I could barely keep up."

"Say anything more about that woman and I will have your tongue as a trophy," Will spits, his back rigid as he looks down his nose at her.

"This tongue keeps your secrets, and it needs to wag to perform magic. So you won't, and I will continue to spit on that woman's grave," she says as she spits on the floor.

His lip pulls into a snarl as his control thins the longer he's in her presence. Her eyes sparkle, and he knows she's goading him. Dragging this encounter out interminably long just to make him suffer. Technically, the dip in magic that exposed them wasn't her fault.

The witch's boorish slurp rips through the quiet house like nails scraping along a chalkboard, and Will represses a shudder.

"You're talking about reincarnation. It's part of the life cycle that no one wants to admit to. As if someone's off-kilter hobbies come from thin air," she says with a shake of her head.

Will's eyes narrow as his mind spins. "Then it's possible that Rebecca's come back and found her way to me."

"As much as I dread such a reunion, yes," the witch says with a shudder. "Souls like yours are bound to find each other again eventually. How old is this woman? I assume it's a woman?"

"Forty, at most."

A body well taken care of, her skin unblemished and unworn, barely any lines around her eyes nor a sag to her flesh. Ehvy appears youthful, bright, and alive. Supple. Will wonders what other parts of her have defied aging.

"You've been away most of her life. The bond only calls when it's close. It likes to pretend it's a chance meeting, an accident. Nothing accidental about it." The teacup clatters on the saucer when she places it on the counter, the impatience in her face clear.

"She looks nothing like Rebecca," Will says, remembering her dark, thick, curly hair and her lush body. The opposite of his love, yet just like her in so many ways. *Does she fuck like Rebecca*, he wonders?

"Not how that works," she says with a wave of her hand as she steps toward him. "It's just the soul that recycles, not the vessel. There won't be a switch that goes off that magically turns her into your dead lover. This woman is her own person, formed by her own experiences and unique. Unfortunately for her, she lost the soul lottery and picked up your lots. She may 'remember' things," the witch says with suspect quotation marks around *remember*, "and she may even have similar interests to the dead woman, but that's where the similarities end."

The way the woman speaks of Rebecca makes Will want to burn down her cottage with her inside. Instead, he takes another deep breath and bites his tongue against his murderous rage. "And if I were to bring her into the fold? Would that disrupt the protections?"

The witch snorts and shakes her head. "The protection is on the land and wrapped around the village, not on you. It's easier to cast on a stationary target. My wards aren't infallible, though, as you well know. Overwhelm the magic, and history may repeat itself. Now I think you have all the information you need, yes?"

Her shrewd reminder of Rebecca's death has his mind churning. Will remembers the witch yelling at him after he buried his love. How gluttonous they were. How they needed more control. The magic couldn't hold. It didn't, and it cost Rebecca her life. A hard lesson to learn, one that forced him to curb his enthusiasm for his bloody luxuries. How he misses them.

There's so much more information he could pull from the witch, but Will has hit his tolerance threshold for her and her home. She confirmed that it's likely Ehvy is some reincarnated version of Rebecca, her essence buried within the depths of the woman who stood before him yesterday. Blood pools at the base of his cock, sending a twitch through his member. As though he's some hormonal teenage boy unable to curb his appetite, the need to fuck is almost unbearable at the mere thought of Ehvy.

"For now," Will says with a sinister smile as he pulls open the door and lets himself out.

The roar of night is loud in his ears, insects and skittering creatures blaring. The onslaught of noise is not enough to ease his aching groin. He sits in his car and shifts himself, trying to ease the pressure, but it does no good. The urge to take her is overwhelming. He can practically feel her hand around his cock, teasing the tip. His eyes roll back into his head before he snaps forward again, growling at himself as he turns the engine over and peels away from the house.

Curses slither across his tongue as he speeds back to Highcombe Nigh, his cock throbbing and in need of release. The essence of her is all-consuming. He wonders if she feels the same as he does, if she thinks of him when she plunges her fingers into her cunt. Does she feel his hands on her? The graze of his teeth across her flesh?

Thoughts of her straddling his dick, her pussy slick and eager as it slides over him, invade his mind. The pleasure on her face as she tears into a throat and paints herself with blood, Will begging to lick off every drop.

"Fuck," he mutters as his cock stiffens more.

He pulls the car around back and enters through the servants' entrance, not wanting any lingering staff to see him in this state. It's embarrassing, this inability to control himself. He's a fucking vampire. Control allowed him to live for a thousand years. Yet here he finds himself on the verge of a waking wet dream.

"I was wondering when you'd get back," comes a purr of a voice as he enters his bedroom.

A beauty sprawls across his massive bed, naked and waiting. She was his release last night after Ehvy and the tour left. Having already received his fill of blood, he needed a fuck. He expected her to be gone by the time he returned from the witch's cottage. Annoyance slithers under his skin, but Will cloaks his face as she stares at him, biting her lip as she pulls herself to sit. Pleasuring himself would have sufficed. Now Will wants blood, too. She had her chance at escape, none the wiser of his true nature. She will not be so fortunate again.

However, he will not soil his sheets. *What to do?*

A sultry smile pulls up his lips as his predator's stare drills into her. Her dampness wafts to him as lust overcomes her face. He doesn't need to use his influence on her, but he does. Just a hint. He wants her wetter than she can get herself. She needs to be frothing. Wild. Oblivious to what he wants to do until it's already done.

The buttons of his shirt clatter and ping off the four-poster bed and a nearby nightstand as he rips his shirt off. His cock leads the way, his need pulsing in his balls as the ache grows unbearable. His eyes beg her to follow him into the bathroom. The shush of her body sliding off the bed mixes with the jingling of his belt buckle as he pulls his pants off, freeing himself of their confines.

Deep into the bathroom sits a stone shower tiled with dark rock to hide his secrets, the drain used to swallowing his needs. *This will do.*

Water sluices through the shower head when he turns it on, and the woman stands behind him when he turns back around. Swollen lips and bed-heavy eyes tell him what she wants, and he will give it to her before he takes the rest.

She grabs his head and presses her lips to his, pushing them both into the massive shower. Knees crack on the floor as she falls in front of him, water cascading down her back as she takes him in her mouth, nearly swallowing him whole. Fingers dig into his thighs as she takes him deep, the depths of her throat wrapping around him and pulling pleasure from his body.

Will groans as he presses a hand to the back of her head, insisting she take more of him. And she does, her lips practically touching his hilt as tears water her eyes. He smiles down at her just as she looks up; he brushes hair away from her face, Ehvy's eyes flashing in place of hers for a moment before disappearing. A groan rises in his throat as he tilts his head back and wallows in the feel of a hot mouth on his cock.

Before the pressure builds to bursting, he pulls himself from her and brings her to her feet. With gentle fingers, he pushes her to the wall as he lowers himself to his knees and buries his face in her cunt. Flat tongue and tip probe her nexus; her hand fists his hair as her orgasm builds. Two fingers find their way inside her as he continues licking and sucking, pushing her to her peak and down again, her cries echoing in the dark shower.

Will smiles into her folds, her sendoff done. Now, it's time for him to finish.

Through pants and gasps, Will keeps licking, flicking her clit with the tip of his tongue as he draws his fingers out and settles her thighs on his shoulders, supporting her weight as she leans into the wall. He glances up to find her eyes closed and her head rolled back, her mouth hanging open as the next wave of pleasure builds.

Good. They taste better when they're fucked to death.

With one arm wrapped around a leg, he dips his face into the thick flesh of her and bites, her body convulsing with the instant orgasm, her screams indiscernible from pleasure or pain. Blood drips down her leg, flowing into his mouth as he drains her life, drawing her deeper into darkness. He uses his persuasion to keep her lust high, to keep her from thrashing until he releases her and sets her feet on the floor.

Her knees buckle, her face far more pallid than it was moments ago, yet she looks even more ready to take him, like he wants to be taken. Or so she thinks.

With one hand wrapped around her neck just tight enough to make her moan, Will's free hand crawls between her legs. One finger probes her opening, burying itself to the knuckle. Then two. Three. The woman's moans grow, and Will ups his vampire persuasion, a fuck drug that keeps her mind from wandering.

Four fingers and her groans grow louder as he plunges into her, her pussy stretching for him.

"More," she mutters, her lips tinted blue as blood pools around their feet with her none the wiser.

Will presses his nose into her ear and says, "How I like when you beg."

He brings his fingers and thumb together and enters her, stretching her. Her legs move wider as his knuckles slide in, and she is his fucking puppet.

"Beg," he whispers as he presses his thumb harder into her throat.

A stuttered 'please' falls from her lips as Will slowly probes her with his fist, her muscles tightening around his wrist as he pushes a little deeper and a little deeper. He dips his head and takes a breast in his mouth, his tongue twirling around the nipple, flicking it before his teeth make their mark. She cries out, and he drives himself deeper, pressing against the limits of her sex before another push tears them asunder.

She yells as he draws from her, blood coating her

stomach as he feeds. His arm pushes further and further until he's buried to his elbow. Choked gurgles rumble in her throat as fat drops hit his face. Blood burbles on her lips and trails down her chin, her eyes blown wide as she looks at him, seeing nothing. Her heart still beats, but barely.

As he pulls himself free of her, blood and viscera falling from her gash and splashing onto the shower floor, Will's nail elongates just enough for him to use the edge to slice up, flaying her from inside to out, her organs exposed past her navel. A sight that makes his still rock-hard cock twitch.

He releases her neck, and she crumples to the ground. A shredded lump of flesh. The pitiful staccato beats of her heart are like wind chimes, desperate and erratic, as her body throws off its last beats of life. Eyelids flutter as his gore-coated fingers wrap around his shaft. Heat still pulses in the blood. The lingering essence of life. He strokes it into himself, reveling in the slick feel of his hand on his shaft, imagining it is Ehvy pleasuring him. Her tongue drags along his throat, licking up the blood from the eviscerated woman. He can feel the press of her lips against his, her smaller hands wrapping around his length, pulling the pleasure from him stroke by stroke.

Blood and water dribble into the V of his groin, and Will takes a hand and mops it up before sticking his fingers in his mouth, savoring the taste of his latest meal. He sighs and throws his head back, his eyes closed as he jerks himself off, the blood creating a squelching noise that he can convince himself is the sultry dampness of Ehvy's cunt wrapped around him as their bodies writhe together.

The pressure builds, his balls tightening as his breaths come in quick gasps, choking him the closer he gets. The world stops, everything goes silent, and Will throws himself forward, his hand catching him on the wall as he gasps and moans, his orgasm pulsing in time with this hand, his load shooting onto the paling legs of his now-expired companion.

His back stiffens as he settles into the high before allowing himself to relax and come down from his peak. He draws his hand up, blood caked within the lines of his palm. Will smiles at the sight, at the pulse of his cock as his orgasm fades and the feelings this strange creature elicits in him. *How dare she?* he thinks. Yet he wants to beg her for more. To have her kneel before him and offer herself up as a sacrifice, turn her into an altar of worship.

It's still early, yet sleep weighs heavily in his eyes. He wants Ehvy in his bed, his body wrapped around her like a duvet, safe in his arms. She will need to change. That much is clear. The blood desire is strong in her if she can smell it in her human form, but she won't be able to consume much in her current state. Rebecca was the same. A lust for blood without the stomach to handle it until Will transformed her.

A smile ticks up his mouth, his fangs catching his lip as he looks at the mess he must now take care of. *All in due time.* He will have her begging for her fate by the time he's done with her.

Chapter Five

EHVY

"My spirits, as in a dream, are all bound up."

E hvy removes the liver from the abdominal cavity and places it on the scale before speaking into the microphone to note her file. A feeling curls in her stomach, and the ghastly images of the car accident outside King's Cross flash through her mind. The phantom smell of blood tickles her senses. A burst of feeling rushes through her, hot and electric, before it disappears entirely.

She clears her throat and pushes the thoughts from her mind, finishing her note. Fingers brush against mottled flesh as she gently lowers the organ back into its rightful place. When her hands are finally free of the body, she rubs her wrist against her nose, replacing the metallic scent with potent antiseptic, and the subtle sweetness of flesh just turned. To someone not used to it, it's a punch to the teeth. But for Ehvy, it's just another day at the office. Another day where blood *doesn't* smell like something she can devour.

Thoughts of Will have infiltrated her mind over the last few days, throwing her out of her rhythm. She's been able to handle victims well enough, but the number of missed Tube stops this week has been embarrassing. Forgetting bags of groceries at the market. Leaving laundry in the washer overnight. Ehvy's no more forgetful than the average person, but ever since Will has taken up residence in her mind, there's hardly room for anything else. It's annoying the hell out of her.

Never has she been so ensorcelled by someone before. How many pretty faces has she seen over the course of her life? None of them left her mind so bubbly—until Will.

The man of her dreams.

Dreams that have skyrocketed over these last few days. His dream image has grown clearer, more intense. More visceral. The touches as if his hands are on her. The smell of blood overwhelming her, sending her mind spinning. She's woken up every day this week gasping, her pussy throbbing as her body lulls after an orgasm she doesn't remember having. It's disturbing, yet more enticing than she'd care to admit. She spends all day fighting these thoughts, only to succumb to them in the night.

No matter how much Ehvy wants her head to go back to normal, she allows Will in, looking forward to their private tour on Thursday. A tour that her friends still don't know about.

Her ears heat as she stares at the corpse, memories of her dream flickering through her mind. The open chest of the victim on the table makes her head swirl, thoughts of fresh blood sending her body throbbing as shame slithers under her skin. She's not a necrophiliac. The body on the slab does nothing for her, even now. It's just more of a trigger. A reminder of Will.

This dead body makes her think of Will.

Anxiety makes Ehvy's teeth chatter as she wraps up, the clock on the wall showing five. A good enough reason to end the day and meet her friends for drinks. She won't be sharing this with them. Not that she shares much about her job, anyway. The scrunched noses and groans of disapproval are enough that she will keep this to herself.

But to mix the handsome man from Highcombe, how a dead body makes Ehvy think of him. Her newfound Pavlovian response to fresh blood and her raucous sex dreams... They would have her committed. That's not to speak of the gruesome history of Will's home and how Will looks remarkably like his ancestor. They don't understand her interests as is. There will be no understanding this desire. They couldn't. She barely does.

Maybe some alcohol will help put things into perspective. It's clear her mind is twisted, like some hormonal teenager eager to get off. It can't have been that long since she last got laid.

It's easy enough to ignore the corpse as Ehvy slides it into the refrigeration unit, locking it when she's done. As if she has to keep it from letting itself out, midsection flayed open, organs falling onto the floor. She scrubs out of the dissection theater, running her hands and arms under the hot water longer than necessary to get any stubborn smell off. It's the subtlety of death that lingers when she leaves work, not the corpse itself. It hangs on her clothes, in her hair, under her nails.

There's a change of clothes in her office, and she spritzes

dry shampoo throughout her tresses to tamp down any less-than-appealing scents. She stuffs her soiled clothes into the bottom drawer of her desk and promises herself she'll take them home tomorrow when she has no additional detours planned.

Ehvy enters the Tube through Monument Station, and as soon as she starts her trek to Bank Station through the underground warren of tunnels, she curses her decision to wear heels. As if she hasn't learned her lesson time and time again. She just wants to look nice. Put together. More adult than she usually feels.

Under Will's gaze, it was like he could see into her soul. Like what she wore on the outside meant little to him. Even though he's the better part of an hour away, the fantastical idea of running into him thrills her. An idiotic notion, but her heels make her feel sexy all the same, despite her cramped toes. The way he looked at her like she was the most delicious thing he's seen... Ehvy wants to *feel* that, and this is one way to do it. Blisters, however, are not remotely sexy.

The heels *click-clack* through the white-tiled tunnels with purpose as she moves with the financial crowd, their day winding down too. Far more men than not, disappointing in this day and age, filter through the tunnels, rushing to get as far away from their offices as possible. Suits of gray and black and navy blend into a tide of monotony. The women stand out more, pops of color in the dreary Underground. An emerald shirt here, yellow pants there.

Then there's Ehvy in her open trench coat, slim pants, and an oversized sweater, costume jewelry hanging down her front and bouncing against her body as she maneuvers through the crowd on her march to the train.

Eyes are on her. She can feel them. Passing men and women glance her way and her desire to feel sexy amplifies. The higher it goes, the more Will flashes through her mind. His angular face painted with a disarming smile, the peek of chest, his well-manicured hands as they wrap around her neck and drag her closer.

Ehvy clears her throat and blinks away the thought, heat flushing her body. Dampness clings under her arms and lingers on the back of her neck, working to push that sexy feeling further away as she tries to think cooling thoughts.

The squeal of the train brakes through the tunnel makes her eyes flutter, and her step falters, the noise sliding into something that could be a scream. Images from her dream flash through her mind. The pale blonde woman. Will. The brakes squeal again, another scream, yet no one reacts to it. The cadence of her heels on the tile builds to a laugh, a resounding cackle keeping the beat of her steps.

Ehvy lifts her hand to wipe away a drip of sweat on her face and gasps. A glove of blood coats her hand, viscous fluid like syrup sliding down her flesh and dripping onto her shoes. A puddle builds on the tile around her feet, reaching out to the suited passersby who pay her no mind. Fear patters her heart, her breathing coming in quick gasps as she stares at her blood-covered hand. Revulsion swirls in her stomach as the sultry sweet smell fills her nose, drowning out the tepid dank scent of the Underground. Memories of Will's study, of the accident, fill her mind and her eyes flutter again as she tries to push them away.

And fails.

Her gums throb with the need to stick her fingers in her mouth and lick them clean, her teeth aching to bite as sickness simmers just underneath the desire. A reminder that this is wrong. It can't be right. Yet nothing feels more perfect.

Eyes bore into the top of her head as people brush past her. When she looks up, it's nothing but a sea of bobbing heads, blank-faced individuals moving like water in the tide, making the one motionless person stand out all the more.

The crowd parts without seeing him. Will stands stock still in the tunnel, hands clasped in front of him as he holds her gaze. He looks much like he did last week, except his hair is tidier and his shirt buttoned. He fits in with this posh crowd more than she does.

Her tongue traces the knife-edged letters of his name as it slices through her mouth, a sound only he can hear. Will smiles—an acknowledgment—as blood flows over his luscious lips. It cascades down his front, covering him from gullet to groin, and Ehvy gasps again. Her breath catches in her chest as she watches his tongue flick out and lick the deluge from his lips. She should be disgusted, traumatized. Yet she can't help but think what that tongue could do to her.

The rush-hour crowd pays them no mind as they blur past the scene, nothing but afterimages of people. There's a pull at her heart, a need to go to him. To get on her knees and offer herself as a tribute to him. She takes a step forward, the disgruntled murmurs of people reaching her ears, yet Ehvy doesn't care what they say. Shoulders and bags bump her, but she doesn't feel them. All the while Will remains stationary, an invisible fixture of the Underground no one else can see.

A copper tang fills her mouth, the sweet taste of blood

coating her tongue. Whatever nausea she felt disappears as she licks her lips, reveling in the flavor. Will's gaze travels down her body and Ehvy follows, finding her front coated in blood. Her body is thick with it, clothes sticking to her flesh as desire thrums through her. The pulsing in her cunt begs her to get off right here in front of God and the financiers.

Train brakes squeal through the tunnel and the noise pierces sense back into her brain. Like a slap, the tunnel comes back into focus. There's no Will. Never was. Ehvy looks down and finds no blood around her feet or down her front. Her hand is just her hand, covered in nothing but her own skin. A salacious taste lingers on her tongue, her gums still throbbing with need, but when Ehvy taps her fingers against her lips, they come back clean. The taste is gone in an instant, just like everything else she just saw and felt.

Anger swells inside her. And shame. She's being stupid, hallucinating a good-looking man in the fucking Tube. She hasn't even texted him, let alone talked to or seen him since Saturday. With a huff she pulls herself together and carries on toward the train, likely to be late at the rate she's moving. She curses her fucking idiocy and shoves Will from her mind. This is her time with her friends and she will have it.

The evening is a struggle to focus, but a couple of drinks help ease the tension from Ehvy's shoulders. She settles into easy conversations with her friends, a quick catch-up that they all take when they can get it. Will hovers in the back of Ehvy's mind the whole time as the ghost of Rebecca whispers sadistic things into her ear. About blood. About Will. Her lithe form, a barely there image in the corner of Ehvy's eye. The woman has followed her from the shadows of Highcombe.

It's going on ten when Ehvy boards the Tube at Oxford Circus, leaving her friends for the evening. The train is empty. Most intelligent people are already home on Tuesday evening. The morning will be rough when she has to wake up for work. At least there's a long weekend to look forward to. Since she'll be taking a sojourn to Highcombe Nigh Thursday evening, she took off on Friday, giving herself the grace to recover from whatever may happen the night before.

Likely nothing.

Now that she's away from her friends and there's nothing else keeping her mind occupied, Will floods back in demanding her attention. Anger and desire war inside of her and she's not sure which one will win.

Street level is quiet when she exits at West Brompton and marches to her apartment. During the week, it's quiet at this time of night. But the silence that settles over her is heavy. Suffocating. It makes the hairs on the back of her neck stand on end.

A burning stare boring into her back prickles her skin, but when she turns, there's no one there. Her heels are thunderclaps on the quiet street, echoing off the brick and blacktop, drawing attention right to her.

Another set of shoes on the sidewalk joins hers, their steps moving in tandem. Ehvy halts at a crosswalk, feigning the need to look before crossing, despite knowing there are no cars to look out for. The shoes walking with her stop too.

Her pulse hammers in her neck, the ringing in her ears roaring as her panic rises. When she walks again, so does the second set of footsteps, matching her stride for stride. She digs her keys out of her handbag and walks faster, the second set of footsteps keeping pace.

She whirls around, ready to confront whoever is following her, however stupid that idea is, even with her keys nestled between her fingers like claws. Except the street is empty. There's no one on the pavement. No one across the street. She's alone.

When Ehvy turns around, something hovers in the shadows of a tree on the other side of the street. Out of reach of a streetlight, it's a perfect spot to hide; she can't tell if someone is there or not. There are no features she can make out, but a darkness thicker than the rest draws her in like a black hole. Her apartment is only a few doors down. She can make it.

Without a second thought, she sprints for her door, her invisible companion giving chase. She imagines a body much bigger than her own slamming into her, tackling her to the ground. A desperate cry squeaks out of her throat as she drives her feet onto the sidewalk, praying her heels hold for a few more feet. She takes the stairs two at a time and enters the passcode for the door faster than she ever has. The door buzzes, the lock clicks—she throws it open and slams it behind her, holding it shut until the telltale click signals it's safe to let go.

Only there's no one running down the street. No one waiting at the bottom of the stoop. No one slamming into the security door. It's just her.

The darkness across the street lingers. A formless void begging her eyes to see something human-shaped as she peers through the glass. The darkness stares back. At her. Into her. There aren't any eyes she can see, but she feels them. She's scared in the way she should be scared. A woman out alone at night, hearing things that may put her in danger. But the longer she watches the dark, the more her fear subsides.

She backs away from the door and makes her way to her apartment. She keeps the lights off when she enters, locking the door behind her. Slashes of moonlight filter through her windows, providing enough light for her to navigate the rooms. From her bedroom, through the sheer curtains, she can still make out the darkness on the far side of the street. Shapeless, featureless, yet she knows it's watching her. It can see her, and her pussy throbs at the thought.

Fear turns to fascination. Then lust. Desire. Ehvy tries to be angry with herself, her body, her libido. Anything. But she's tired of fighting. Exhausted with keeping herself in check.

Fuck it.

Like a floodgate crashing open, her pulsing need from earlier—from seeing Will—if only in her head, comes roaring back. Whatever lingering fear from her run down the street evaporates, replaced by an overwhelming desire to climax.

Ehvy throws her bag onto a nearby chair along with her coat. It's not possible for the figure outside to see her, but she can feel its gaze. *Like Will's gaze from the Tube.* She can't help but think they feel the same. Her breathing grows ragged as she pulls her shirt over her head and throws off her bra. Heels clatter against the wood floor as she kicks them off, then peels off her pants and underwear, soaked through with her desire.

On hands and knees, she crawls onto her bed with her eyes on the window, knowing the darkness can see her. It's not him. She knows it's not.

There's no one there.

Can't be.

Yet she feels Will's gaze—that penetrating stare that hides centuries of knowledge in such a youthful body—rove over her naked form as she lies back on the bed as the outside world fades away.

Her fingers drag down her lip and she imagines them being Will's, blood-coated and slick, sliding down her with ease as she licks the viscous fluid away. It should disgust her. Such a kink never interested her. Yet Will in the tunnel covered in blood, her body smeared with it, makes her cunt throb and swell with need.

One hand finds her breast and twists a nipple.

Harder.

It's little more than a breath, a noise that could be the wind through a crack or a flicker in her head. She twists the sensitive peak, sending a slice of pain into her chest. Her breath shudders as her other hand ventures lower.

She imagines Will sliding through her window like smoke, his gaze penetrating her before his cock does. The hard planes of his chest, the V of his hips pointing toward something she desperately wants inside of her.

Her fingers find a drenched cunt, needy and waiting to be fucked. Two fingers slide in easily and she arches her back, trying to drive them further inside as her fingers move to the rhythm her body craves. She turns her head and greets a flutter of lips pressing into her neck. The ghost of a face, of a nose at her cheek as lips grace her collarbone. The space next to her remains cold, yet her skin sears as she thinks of Will settling beside her.

The phantom face presses into her neck as Ehvy digs her

nails into her breast, pinching the skin and sending flashes of pleasure to her core. A weight settles over her probing hand, a weight separate from hers. Her eyes flash open, but she is alone, pleasuring herself as she pictures a man she just met days ago.

Yet the weight remains.

Like a hand has nestled itself on top of hers, invisible to her eyes as phantom fingers slide over her own to tease at her opening. Her mind is lost, unmoored, wanting to bite, to grab onto something, but it's just her. First one finger slides into her, then a second, filling her to bursting as the digits move in tandem, the phantom following her pulsing rhythm as Ehvy pleasures herself.

It's impossible. There's no one else here, yet her fingers are not the only ones inside of her.

She presses her head back into her pillow, moans choking her as what could only be a hand wraps around her throat and gives her a gentle squeeze. The two sets of fingers probe her, fuck her like she couldn't fuck herself, until her body gives in to the feeling and her walls clench around them, trying to draw them deeper.

The willowy presence of Rebecca flickers before her, moonlight slicing through her body as she stands at the foot of Ehvy's bed. An open robe exposes small, pert breasts, nipples dark against ghostly white skin. Rebecca's hand disappears below the point of pubic hair, plunging her fingers into her cunt in a rhythm that matches Ehvy's own.

Pleasure builds as Ehvy fucks herself, delirious with desire as tingles make their way down her body and pool in her pussy. A blood-splattered windshield flashes through her mind.

Building.

Screams of pain.

Building.

The cloying metallic scent of blood filling the air.

Until everything goes silent and her body explodes. The rush of blood from her head is so intense she nearly blacks out, her pussy throbbing around her fingers, filled more than she could possibly be. She chokes on her moans as she rides the orgasm to a lull. Her body is spent, her mind in shambles, yet she feels deeply satiated.

Whatever forbidden door the mere sight of Will has unlocked in Ehvy frightens her. The blood. The gore. The desire it builds within her. Never has she felt like this. Then again, never has she felt so driven toward another person.

She pants as she comes down from her sexual high. Whatever phantom was next to her has departed, if there was any there at all. The apparition of Rebecca fucking herself at the foot of her bed is gone. She feels like she's breaking, unraveling. Like Will has picked at a wound she didn't know she had, and now it won't stop bleeding.

She should want it to stop. Ehvy shouldn't feel like this about these things. About Will. It makes no sense. Perhaps it's something she should embrace. So much of her life has been sensible. Logical. Stiff. Will is the Valium allowing her to relax, easing her muscles and lulling her to sleep.

Ehvy's eyelids grow heavy with the thought of him, and she sighs as she pulls the duvet over her. He is the flame that she should pull her hand away from. Instead, she wants to walk right into the fire.

Chapter Six

EHVY

*"I might call him a thing divine, for nothing
natural I ever saw so noble."*

Ehvy wipes her clammy hands on her pants again. The damn things are little more than slick pools the closer she gets to Highcombe Nigh. She texted yesterday to confirm that this entire trip wasn't a lark. She half-expected not to hear from Will. That he didn't mean what he said, and she's been trying not to obsess all week.

Until his response came—he was looking forward to her visit.

That's that, then.

The trip gnaws at her mind the entire train ride in. What could Will want with *her*? What does he see in *her*? And what does Ehvy see in him other than his appearance? She guesses this is the trip to learn that. Who he is—what he is— where he's been. Does he have monsters in his family tree?

Who was the William Sandridge married to Rebecca? Because it certainly wasn't the Will she's meeting now. That's impossible.

Ridiculous, even.

What's truly ridiculous is that Ehvy didn't tell anyone where she was going. How many true crime stories start this way? But something kept snatching the words away every time she tried to mention Will. Something deep inside told her to keep him to herself. Something that sounded distinctly feminine and brutal, a whisper of a voice that stroked a feeling of familiarity down her spine with a cold, dead finger. No one was ready for him yet.

Hell, she's not ready for him. But that bandage is about to be ripped right off.

Will's very presence haunted her all week, lingering in the shadows, lurking in the crevices of her mind and deep within her soul. It's been an effort to get through the work-week, to focus on the tasks at hand. If it wasn't Will's face playing games in her mind, it was the sly face of the long-dead Rebecca Sandridge or the common-sense thoughts that kept trying to break through. The tiny voice at the back of her mind has been quiet but insistent.

Don't do this.

Something telling her that there would be no turning back after this.

The drive to the manor is winding, the trip more jostling now that the surrounding landscape is black. The closer the cab carries her, the tighter the trees cave in, wrapping her in their claustrophobic arms. So close their leaves practically brush against the glass. Something tickles Ehvy's cheek and she whips her head around to find herself alone in the back seat. Her heart thundering, she rubs her hands on her knees and releases a shuddering breath.

Calm.

Little more than the whisper of the wind into her ear, brushing across her neck. It makes the little hairs stand on end in the most terrifyingly delectable way. A weight presses into her knee as Ehvy's hands sit knotted in her lap. Her core throbs at the touch and she bites into her tongue to keep herself present. In the corner of her eye, willowy hair made of starlight shimmers in the darkness, but it's gone as soon as Ehvy looks. The low crack of a cackle breaks the quiet of the cab, the noise blending into the pop of gravel under the tires as the cab rolls to a stop.

"Your name then?" the cabbie asks.

"Ehvy," she says, swallowing her anxiety and desperately trying to brush away the haunting presence of a long-dead woman, tells the driver her name. They sit quietly in the rumbling car for far too long before a resounding click sounds over the dark landscape. The wrought-iron gate opens, the lane yawning wide in front of them. The round-about in front of the main entrance opens like arms, the fountain in its center still spewing water with no one around to see it.

The manor itself is made of shadows, the lighted windows struggling to break free of the night falling around it. In the daylight, it's merely another rich home squatting on a hill. But now as it looms over Ehvy the closer the cab gets, it's a living thing reaching out to her, anxious to sink its teeth into her supple flesh and swallow her down. And here she is, about to dive straight into the mouth of the beast.

Ehvy lurches with the car as it rolls to a stop, the driver

saying nothing as she taps her card on the reader and pays the fare. She issues a quiet "thank you" before letting herself out. The car rolls away before the door closes, the momentum landing it home as the tail lights illuminate the night like eyes staring at her in the dark.

How will she leave? Now that she watches the cab depart, her heart flutters at the abandonment as reality crashes back in—she is stranded. She pulls her phone out of her purse and sighs when she finds a full signal; her ability to call for a cab remains. It's little consolation, having just been dropped off at a stranger's manor, but it's something. Her location services are on. She may not have told her friends where she's going, but Ehvy will use technology to fill in the gaps.

There's an effort to her outfit this evening. Something far more put together than when she was last here, but she hopes it's still muted. A pair of form-fitting black pants and heels, a blouse that reveals just a peek of cleavage, and a sensible blazer. It's still only Thursday evening, not a rousing Saturday night. She wants to look sharp, not on the hunt.

Although the notion that she's already captured her prey flits through her mind, and she jerks to a stop. That Will would be prey is laughable. Where the thought comes from, she has no idea, but it feels right, despite the fact that she hadn't been looking to capture anything at all.

Gas lamps flicker along the driveway and Ehvy wonders if they're really gas or some modern invention made to look like the original. Either way, they do little to press back the weight of darkness that's settled across the estate in the night. Gloom wrapped the manor like a shroud the last time she was here. Now the historical home looms like a specter, the darkness a void from which she will never return if she ventures too far.

The estate looks much smaller at night. That should make it less formidable, yet her knees quake as she mounts the steps to the front door, not knowing where else to go. Will never gave her explicit instructions, and doubt creeps into her again, despite his own confirmation. Maybe his offer was empty after all. She wasn't supposed to take him up on it. She's a fool to travel an hour by rail, plus another ten minutes by cab in the middle of the week.

Windows stare down at her, judging her as she comes closer. Soft light winks through half-draped curtains while people move about the rooms, giving the manor a lived-in feel. She half expects tours to still be going on, yet there are no buses in the roundabout or cars in the parking lot. So it must be the staff. And Will.

As Ehvy places her foot on the top step, the beating of her heart nearly overwhelms her. Her head swims and the ground around her swirls in blacks and greens with slashes of reds and violets, flowers overflowing from their pots. Their cloying scent suffocates her, wrapping around her lungs and pouring into her nose. She clears her throat and presses her fingers to her forehead as she closes her eyes against the onslaught.

This was a mistake. A stupid, stupid mistake. She shouldn't be here.

As she turns, the door pulls open, the hinges giving a slight squeak as the massive wooden barrier peels away to reveal a softly lit foyer and an older gentleman in a sharp suit with his hand on the knob.

"Miss Ehvy, I presume?" he says in an accent that speaks

of a life lived around the elite, low and drawn out. His eyes sparkle with youth, a contrast against his lined face and white hair, his pate wispy. "Master Sandridge is expecting you. This way, please."

He motions into the foyer and heat flushes Ehvy's neck and face. She silently praises the shadows, hoping they hide whatever blush may be creeping across her skin. Will expects her. Of course. He said he would be. Maybe this isn't a mistake after all.

Delicate heels sound thunderous in a foyer that feels expansive. She didn't appreciate it the last time she was here, but the entryway is vast. It seemed smaller when it was filled with people. Now it's just her and her escort. Shadows dance across the paintings that line the walls, eyes staring down at her, watching her walk through their ancestral home.

The butler—valet?—leads her across the foyer and past the hallway she first traversed what feels like an eternity ago. The one that led her to Will. The haunting scent that warmed his study fills her nose for a moment before fading away, a reminder of what was there. She stares down the corridor, the rope still in place. Something pulls her in that direction, begging her to walk the same path. Except her escort guides her elsewhere.

He moves aside another rope to let her through, and Ehvy can't help but wonder how tedious that must get. Or perhaps the space Will and the staff occupy works around the trappings of the tours and it's no issue at all.

Another corridor greets her, much like the last. Lit in a mix of flickering candles and soft electric lights, it seems inviting while shadows collect in corners like cobwebs. More paintings line the walls, ancestors watching over their property from beyond the grave.

They pass another portrait of Rebecca. Her waist is no longer cinched; her hair bobbed. From the twenties, likely. She wouldn't have been a bright young thing then. Too old. Yet something tells Ehvy that wouldn't have stopped Rebecca from trying. And William would have encouraged it. Without knowing that truth, Ehvy feels it in her gut.

As if to validate her thoughts, the portrait winks, drawing Ehvy up short. She stares at the canvas for a moment, waiting for the trick to happen again. But the painting remains stationary. Nothing but colors swirled into the resemblance of a dead woman. A light laugh slides through Ehvy's ears and she flinches. She gives Rebecca's portrait one more glance and continues after her escort.

Ehvy steps lightly on the runner, fighting some deep-rooted fear that she doesn't belong. Her surroundings exude wealth, a wealth she's never had a dream of obtaining through her medical examiner's career. What she has makes her happy. However, Will would make her happier.

Frustration and anger well within her. Stupid flights of fancy that flutter in her head, making her think such stupid things. She barely knows him beyond his name and the scant information her internet sleuthing turned up. How can she possibly know that this stranger will make her happy?

A sitting room, much like those she's seen in period dramas, stands beyond the open door as her escort steers her inside. The vaulted ceilings rise high overhead, garish turn-of-the-century wallpaper reaching up the sides of the room to touch art deco styling swirling across the ceiling. Flames roar from the fireplace, spitting soft light at nearby furniture that beckons her to sit. Two wine glasses and a bottle rest on a silver tray atop a sideboard; her escort motions to the display.

"Do you like red?" he asks as he reaches for the bottle.

Words flee her tongue. The room, her escort, the ready-to-serve wine are all so overwhelming. She nods, and he pours her a glass as if he were a sommelier at a fine restaurant. The liquid barely moves as he holds it out to her and she takes it, a whiff of alcohol hitting her nose.

"Please make yourself comfortable. Master Sandridge will be with you shortly." He gives her a tight smile and a curt bow before turning heel and leaving her in this grand sitting room feeling woefully underdressed.

Ehvy should sit, make herself comfortable, but her blood feels effervescent, making her far too twitchy to stay in one place. Lips meet cold glass as she takes a sip. The wine is a dry, sweet vintage; she won't pretend she can guess its provenance. It glides across her tongue, waking up her palette before it slides down her throat, sending warmth to her fingers and cheeks.

Her feet carry her around the room, her fingers dancing along the mantle of a fireplace the size of a pantry. Detailed carvings frame the flames, hand-hewn and speaking of interminable age. The people it's seen over the centuries must be innumerable and fuel for all the gossip she found on High-combe Nigh during her search.

A search that returned a sordid history of the Sandridge family with hints of something otherworldly. Fodder for some horror novel, maybe. Not reality. Ehvy curses how flighty her mind is and takes another sip of wine.

In the corner, away from the fire, is a fainting couch

stuffed to the gills under antique patterned cloth. Ehvy sits and runs her free hand along the seat, imagining all the people who have sat here. Her fingers grace the arm and the world around her flickers, the haunting cadence of voices brushing her ears; her hand becomes someone else's, with rings and bracelets and blood-red nails. In a flash it's her hand again, plain, unpainted, with meager jewelry compared to what she just saw.

A laugh, trilling like breaking glass, draws her attention as the room of today and the room of yesterday flicker in overlapping images, her eyes hopping from one to the other. Ghosts from the past haunt the room, their essence stamped into the fibers of it, moving through time. Reaching out to her. She can't see their faces, but one body reminds her of who she is in her dreams.

Rebecca.

The cascading starlight of her hair, her slender fingers. The same fingers she just saw. Her tall, lean frame. Ehvy sees the body in front of her, but when she looks down, Rebecca's nightdress of pure silk wraps around her own legs, the glass in her hand heavy with something more than wine. Thicker than wine, leaving legs along the inside of the glass heartier than any red she's seen.

A door clicks and suddenly the room is just a room, the fire in the fireplace heating her face, the wine in her hand barely touched. She is just Ehvy in her modern clothes, not someone from the past luxuriating in their finery. There is no past in her present. She is merely in a sitting room in an old manor, the guest of its owner. Heat flashes through her, making her senses swirl.

The door creaks and she stands, her muscles twitching as she scrambles to get a hold of her wits.

Run.

One foot lifts imperceptibly, little more than her muscle shuddering, before she puts it back down. A knee-jerk reaction. Panic. She doesn't belong here.

She doesn't want to run. Not really. Not as the tall frame of the man she barely knows comes through the door, his eyes roving the far side of the sitting room, cascading over his belongings before landing on her.

Air leaves the room. Her heart stops beating. Somewhere, someone screams and Ehvy's eyes flutter, but she shakes the noise away. Her mind is playing tricks on her yet again. Highcombe Nigh is playing tricks. As if Will swims inside her head, riling up the calm water there.

"Ehvy. I'm so glad you could make it."

The amiable smile that glides across his face could stop the earth from spinning. The way he looks at her with deep ocean-blue eyes, desperate and grasping, thankful for her presence but also pinned. Eager. Anxious. Nervous, even.

Like a flip book, the emotions pass across his face faster than Ehvy can process them, there and gone in less than a blink. Until it's just him. Will walks toward her much the same way he did when they first met. Only now his suit is complete, heather gray with black wing tips, the Oxford underneath unbuttoned at the collar and his tie nowhere to be found. His unbuttoned jacket frames his body. Will's hair is immaculate, shaped into a fine wave across his head. Where last time he looked frazzled, now he's composed and Ehvy can't take her eyes off of him.

This is why she's here. Whatever doubt, whatever apprehension she had, dissolves as Will's eyes devour her.

She's glad this isn't a joke. Time enough for that yet, she supposes, but like all things that have happened to her over this last week, her gut tells her no.

This is no joke.

Her gut is also telling her to run.

While she still can.

Another scream sounds from somewhere deep within her, but this time she doesn't flinch. She smiles as Will moves toward her, his hand out. Reaching. Waiting.

Run.

But just behind the voice of reason, there's the devilish lilt of lips at her ear adding, *to him.*

She listens, moving closer to him, into his orbit, and allows him to absorb her. Her fingers brush his palm as they wrap around his warm hand. The heat of his flesh on hers shoots electricity through her body, straight to places that have no business being riled up right now.

Yet here she is.

"Thank you for inviting me, Will. I've been looking forward to this," she says, her voice breathy.

She tried not to. Tried to live her life without thoughts of Will overwhelming her, but it's been impossible. Ehvy's been looking forward to this more than she'd care to admit. More than she wants him to know.

Chapter Seven

WILL

"...tell your piteous heart there's no harm done."

Ehvy is decadently sweet, like rich chocolate that can poison the body, yet he will devour her whole. When his eyes land on her, there is no turning away. She rests her hand in his and he could dissolve into so much bubbling flesh. Somehow, he remains standing. If this night could never end, it would be too soon.

"I hope it wasn't too much trouble getting here. To be honest, I'm surprised you came, despite your text," he says, laying the truth bare.

Will would rather eat the wine glass than admit out loud that he fretted about her arrival all week, whether she would show or if the distrust of the modern world would dissuade her. Anyone would need to be careful in these uncertain times; there are many monsters lurking in the shadows. He should know. He's one of them.

Ehvy laughs, the wine in her glass swaying as she watches

him, eyes tracing and cataloging his every movement. Will can practically feel her mind etching him into her memory. It's a laugh distinct to the creature in front of him, but the way her teeth flash between her lush lips, how her head tilts —the ghost of Rebecca lingers under the surface.

"I doubt that. With a place like this and all your other business ventures, I'm sure you were too busy to give me a second thought," she volleys back with a light shake in her voice. Pink warms her cheeks, and she takes a hurried sip of wine.

She's nervous. Good. She should be. It appears this modern world did wriggle its way in, after all. She must have looked him up. There isn't much available on this current iteration of Will Sandridge. Everything else is little more than fables to a logical mind like hers.

Her lips wrap over the edge of the glass as she sips. The thought of those lips wrapping around him makes the room spin.

"My days are busy," he says with a low chuckle as he walks toward the wine. "My nights are less so."

His gaze wants to linger, but he won't let it. Still, the image of Ehvy carves itself into his mind by her very nails. She leaves her hair down, thick and tumbling over her shoulders in ringlets he wants to twist around his fingers. Her clothes are shapelier this evening as they settle across luscious curves and dip low enough to give him a peek of what she keeps hidden from the world. She is in every way the opposite of his lost love, far sturdier than Rebecca ever appeared. Yet her hesitance, tinged with curiosity, is an ache of familiarity in his mind. An itch brews in his palm—the need to touch, absorb—but he replaces the need with a glass and faces her.

"Come," he says. "You're here for a private tour. Let me at least satisfy my end of our bargain."

A wet tongue slides across his lips just before he takes a sip, watching her walk toward the door.

"I still don't believe this is real," Ehvy says with an anxious laugh. "Like I'll wake up and this will have been an elaborate dream."

Ehvy waits on the other side of the door for him as Will walks up beside her, increasing their proximity. Removing the air between them. She takes a shuddering breath when he's near and he has to hide the smile that wants to bloom on his face.

"I have nothing but the noblest intentions, I assure you." A member of staff walks past the end of the corridor and Will motions to them. "I promised there would be staff on site."

If only Ehvy knew how he defined "noble intentions." No doubt she would not think so, but to him they are the noblest. The smile that haunts the corner of her mouth makes him want to reach out and touch it. The sparkle in her eyes every time she looks at him begs him to fall into them. All the ancient willpower of his centuries of life prevents him from throwing her against the wall and taking her right here. His cock twitches at the thought, but he takes another sip of wine and sends calming thoughts through his body.

Not yet.

"Already you're doing a better job than the docent,"

Ehvy says with a laugh as she raises her glass. "Perhaps you should do the tours. You won't lack visitors that way."

Her cheeks flame as she realizes what she just said and laughs nervously before taking a large gulp of her wine. Will huffs, knowing she hopes he didn't take what she said how she said it, but he is. He's attractive and he would draw crowds if he were giving the tours.

"I don't like crowds much, unfortunately. And after a while, they wouldn't like me." A tight smile screws up his face and Ehvy nods with an uncertain expression, not understanding what he's trying to say. It's a vagueness he plans to keep in place. "Managing this estate and my other real estate investments occupies enough of my time as it is. What about you? What job did I take you away from this evening?"

Will tips his glass to his mouth as Ehvy clears her throat and says, "I'm a medical examiner."

Wine sucks into the back of his throat and Will sputters as he tries to process what she just said. Such a gruesome job for anyone, let alone the pretty thing at his side. Perhaps more of Rebecca is in her than he originally thought.

"That's too much, isn't it?" Ehvy says with a wince. "My friends warn me not to drop that bomb too quickly, but I find it better to just rip the bandage off, yeah? If that scares someone away, then they aren't worth keeping around. I'm not about to find another job to suit someone with a weak stomach."

Longing eyes look at him. Hopeful. A little afraid that, like so many others, she's run him off with her macabre career choice. Fortunately for Ehvy, it's done quite the opposite.

"Forgive me," Will says with one more cough. "No, that doesn't scare me in the slightest. It was just entirely unexpected and, dare I say, refreshing." He clears his throat and returns her look with something soothing, hoping she reads him accurately.

Now it's Ehvy's turn to choke on a laugh. "Refreshing? You're the first to say that about cutting up dead bodies for a living."

"It's different though, isn't it?" He motions around a corner and Ehvy follows as he brings them deeper into the manor. Will's supposed to be showing her around, yet she seems content just wandering the corridors, speaking to him. "Can't say I've run into too many medical examiners in my life." Not recently, anyway. "How did you decide on that career path?"

Red still tinges the tops of her cheeks like she's in a permanent blush; Will longs to brush his hand along her face, feeling her flesh beneath him. Her hand has just been a taste, and his tongue wants so much more.

"I always found anatomy fascinating, but people less so. There's a measure of peace with the dead, and when there are questions I'm tasked with answering, it allows me to focus and listen to what their bodies tell me." His silence must extend longer than he intended because she looks at him and winces. "*That's* a bit much, isn't it?"

"Not at all," he says with a smile, fighting to keep his hand from gravitating to the small of her back. His body is eager to get closer, to pour over her. "You must have enjoyed the more fanciful history of the manor, then."

She laughs into her wine glass, nearly empty now.

"People back then never really knew what they were looking at. Something as simple as tuberculosis was enough to send people spiraling into the supernatural."

"Indeed. Here." Will opens a nearby door into a ballroom that's sat unused since women were barely out of corsets. The pang of Rebecca's memory overwhelms him as he gazes into the dark room, but he pushes forward and turns on a nearby switch.

Lights flutter to life, illuminating the massive ballroom in a dull, dusty haze. Motes flitter through the air as Ehvy coughs and Will second guesses whether opening up the room was a good idea.

"I apologize. This room's been under lock and key for longer than I realized," he says with a frown, taking in the blanketed furniture and dance floor covered with a thick layer of dust.

The moons of her eyes speak to something else entirely. She's enraptured as her gaze flits over the room as if she's watching something he can't see. Ehvy looks up and takes in the gilt frescoed ceiling. A commission by Rebecca once the turn of the Edwardian era loomed. It was to be the beginning of her remodel to match the more Art Deco style that was becoming popular. She never finished it, resulting in an anachronistic room that pained him to even open the doors. So he didn't. He ordered the room shut up and when the tours began, he did not include it on the route.

"It feels..." Ehvy waggles her hand in front of her, trying to find the words. "Unfinished. The walls and ceiling don't match, right?" She motions between the two, pointing out the obvious stylistic differences.

Will gives her a tight smile, hoping it doesn't look too severe; the pain in his heart is sharp, and it's hard for him to get through it.

"You're correct. The last true mistress of the house died before she could finish it. Perhaps you've seen her portrait." He swallows and wraps his fingers around the doorknob as Ehvy shifts closer to him while still staring into the ballroom.

Her eyes narrow and then go wide. "The thin woman with pale hair. Rebecca."

She seems to lose focus for a moment as if something comes to mind that Will can't see. It lasts only a moment before she blinks and finds his gaze.

"I believe so, yes." His eyes flick around the ballroom once again, his face serious, before he looks at the woman next to him. "Before my time, of course."

A frown flutters across her eyebrows as Ehvy stares at him. Into him. Her lips part, the bottom lip full and begging to be bitten. The way she looks at him, dissecting him with her gaze, is unnerving. Like she knows. Or perhaps suspects. Except that's not possible. Even if she does suspect, she looks almost...inquisitive. Over the course of their quick investigation of the ballroom, their bodies have drifted closer together. Ehvy's shoulder sits at his chest; the heat of her pulsing into him begs him to wrap his arms around her.

Will clears his throat and says, "Let me show you something." Their bodies brush against each other as he turns off the light and closes the ballroom door. "Would you like more wine?"

Ehvy shakes whatever thoughts she had out of her head as she smiles and he takes the wine glass from her, brushing her fingers with his. A jolt flashes through him, an image of Rebecca's visage melding with Ehvy's sultry face swirling in his mind. His lost love hasn't occupied his thoughts this much in ages. All he wants to do is reach out and hold on to Ehvy—this reborn version of Rebecca—and not let go.

Whatever reservations she has, she's staying with him, at least for now. He hasn't run her off. Time enough for that, perhaps. Or maybe, she'll accept him for what he is and become what she's meant to be.

Will places their glasses on a waiting tray as they pass a table. Perhaps this next part of their private tour will be too much. It will require more trust than what she's already giving him, and he's not sure if this will push her fragile boundaries too far.

There are things she knows about him. That much is clear. What's clearer still is what she suspects of him. If she's researched the manor, she's likely stumbled upon old pictures of an ancestor of Will's that looks remarkably like him. There are rational enough explanations for that, but he sees the war of irrationality in her eyes. The questions she can't help but think. It could be why she's humoring him, to prove to herself that he is nothing but an ordinary human. It's why, despite her hesitation, he knows she won't deny him what he wants to show her.

"Where are we going?" she asks after a moment of silence, following him deeper into the manor.

He looks over his shoulder with a sly smile and says, "You'll see."

At the back of the manor, where the carpet is less worn from the lack of feet treading upon it, is a thick wooden door barred with steel. A simple latch lifted will open it, but he advised the staff to never go down there unless instructed. It's off-limits for everyone save for him—and now Ehvy.

The steel clunks as he lifts the lever and pulls the door open. Its hinges are silent—well-oiled and used. Thinking she's right behind him, he steps onto the pitch-black landing and pulls a lantern from the wall. With a turn of a switch, it flares to life, lighting him up along with the damp-looking stones behind him. Yet when he turns, she stands out of arm's reach. Her hands knot together as her gaze takes in the door, worry etching lines around her tense mouth. Will's heart sinks as doubt creeps into his veins. There was never any doubt about Rebecca, not when she faced the darkness. But Ehvy hesitates and he can't help the skipped beat of his heart.

"We'll leave the door open, and we'll only be down there a moment. It's not nearly as terrifying as it looks," Will says, holding out his hand.

It's far worse. But she won't be seeing those parts just yet.

She looks at war with herself; her face twisting as she mulls the prospect over. Deep down, she must know not to go into the strange man's basement. There are documentaries outlining the fallacies of doing things such as this. And with due merit. But not now. He won't allow any harm to come to her.

Resolve washes over her, like she just put her foot down in an argument with herself. Ehvy huffs, squaring her shoulders, and walks toward him. Fear still flickers in her eyes, but she's stubborn and more than willing to follow him. Doubt dissolves and Will breathes a sigh of relief.

Excellent.

"Give me your hand. The stairs are steep and there's only one lantern," Will says, his hand out to her.

Ehvy stares at it for a moment before settling her gaze on his face, taking his hand and wrapping her fingers around his. The heat of her overwhelms him as images of Rebecca flash through his mind. It's almost too much, but he comports himself as he steps down the stairs, guiding her to the basement of the manor.

To his surprise, she doesn't let go when they hit the stone at the base of the stairs. Instead, she shifts her hand and threads their fingers to hold on tighter. Fantasies of pinning her against the stone wall and taking her right here make him smile. He's thankful for the darkness hiding his face.

The smell hits him before he can react, and he wonders how Ehvy will respond. Blood sits thick in the air, his personal stores tucked behind one of the closed doors. Doors that he will not be opening tonight. Instead, their destination is farther down where a door gapes, the room unused.

"That smell," Ehvy says, her voice prickling Will's skin. "What is it?"

"It's damp down here. Moisture and dirt, perhaps?" he lies, knowing full well that's not what she smells.

He peeks over his shoulder and watches her sniff the air and turn her head each way, trying to find the source. The same way she did when she stumbled into his study that fateful day. No, he is not in the wrong showing her the ball-room or this fanciful little cell that's been sitting in this manor for five hundred years, at least. It was newer when Rebecca came into his life and heavily used after it.

She lets him guide her into a circular room, manacles on the floor and dangling from the ceiling. The stale tang of copper sits heavy in the air. As Will draws the lantern in front of them, the light reflects off more steel—a selection of indiscernible implements against a wall. An unused table sits in the center of the room, crusted and dirty. They're so quiet, a steady drip taps a rhythm into his ears.

"A dungeon," Ehvy whispers, almost reverent.

"Perhaps. Actual use has been lost to time," Will says with a smirk, knowing full well that's a lie.

Ehvy gasps, and a throaty laugh escapes her. "You were right, Will."

His name on her lips nearly sets him ablaze. It's the finest music, a symphony of sound. If only she would say it to him forever.

He smiles, then frowns as he faces her, hoping his look is playful. "About what?"

Ehvy's teeth shine in the low light of the lantern as she returns his smile. "This was absolutely worth my while."

Her hand squeezes his, a silent assurance that he is walking the right path with her. Their interests align more than he could have hoped for. Still, with Rebecca, there was no coaxing. Her bloody desires rested at the surface, notions she had to hide until Will gave her the permission she needed. With Ehvy, her desires are latent or outright denied. He'll have to ply her open gently, allowing her to accept what he knows is simmering deep within her.

Something shifts in a nearby cell, and he hopes it is too quiet for Ehvy to hear, but her head turns toward the sound.

"What was that?" she asks, her face pointing down the corridor where he will not take her.

Yet.

"Our sign to return to the civilized areas of the manor. While I pay for a routine exterminator, his reach seems to elude the vermin that call this section of the estate home. Such is the bane of a cellar like this," Will says, hoping she buys the excuse.

If the wrinkle of her nose is anything to judge by, he needn't worry. Their hands stay locked together as he guides her out of the dungeons and to the too-bright main floor of the manor. Ehvy laughs and presses her hand to her chest as she watches Will close the door. He laughs with her, thinking about the close call with his blood stores nearly ruining their fun. He is winning her, but that would have been too much too soon.

The rest of the evening, they peel back the layers of their lives as he walks her through the bedrooms of the roped-off upper floors, the playrooms, the music room, a library. Ehvy marvels at what he shows her and asks probing questions, desperate to dig into the history of the house and him. He is just as eager as she is, and they talk for hours, time slipping away in a blur of excited conversation.

Something must register in Ehvy's beautiful head because, for the first time all evening, she pulls her cell phone from her purse and curses.

"I've missed the last train. Shit. I didn't realize it was so late."

She purses her lips as she flicks through her phone's screen, likely looking up a cab or rideshare, which will take ages and cost her a horse if she were to use one all the way out here.

He can ask her to stay. Horribly forward, but there's

space enough for her to maintain a sense of safety. Or if she doesn't feel the need for such space...

No. It's too soon. Not for any ridiculous notion of propriety. He's seen the way she looks at him. It would be an offer gladly taken. She's just not quite ready for the fucking he wants to give her. A little more time. Peel a few more layers and she will be his for the taking. And he, hers.

"My driver will take you back," Will says without missing a beat.

Ehvy blusters and scoffs. "That's ridiculous. I mean, thank you. But no. I couldn't. It's too far and he'll be out terribly late."

"He's a valet, not a schoolboy," Will says with a laugh that cracks a smile across Ehvy's worried face. "And it will give me peace of mind to know you got home safe."

She looks at him with a watery smile before looking at her hands. "Thank you. I must pay you back for this. It's too much otherwise."

"Nonsense. You'll do no such thing. Unless..." A sly look comes over Will's face and Ehvy looks skeptical, albeit a bit intrigued. "You let me take you to dinner in London this weekend. You can repay me with more of your time."

She chuckles, a breathy thing that sends shivers across his skin. "Fair trade, I think. You have my number. Feel free to use it."

Ehvy brings him more joy than he's had in ages. Her mere presence warms him in ways he hasn't felt since Rebecca. She is everything he hoped she would be—and so much more. Time apart from her will be torture.

Will calls his valet to bring the car around. As it idles in front of the fountain, Ehvy looks at him, her eyes wicked, her mouth begging as she thanks him for a wonderful evening. The desire to tuck her abundant hair behind her ear and run his thumb along her jaw makes his skin itch with need. But he composes himself. Only a few days and he will see her again.

As she's walking down the stairs toward the waiting car, she stops halfway, her back stiff. Will frowns as she stands there, not sure what's come over her. Just as he's about to call to her, to ask if she's forgotten something, he hears her mutter 'fuck it' before she turns and marches back to him.

Ehvy's hands reach out, fingers grazing his cheeks as she pulls his face to hers; their lips crash into each other in divine will. His arms snake around her body and pull her into him as she holds his face, her lips pressing into his. She opens her mouth, the tip of her tongue teasing before he lets her in, deepening their kiss.

It's an exquisite pause in time as they stand entangled, drinking each other in. The longing in him, the desire, rages like an inferno. He could fuck her on these stairs, but he uses all the control he can muster to fight against it, refusing to ruin this glorious moment.

After an eternity in her embrace, she pulls away, searing cold slicing between them. But she's smiling and Will is stunned but smiling as well. This time he tucks hair behind her ear and holds her face in his hand as the other keeps hold of her back.

"Goodnight, Will," she says before she pulls away and enters the car.

The gates open as the valet drives her around the fountain. Any other man wouldn't be able to see, but he can as she turns around and stares at him while the car disappears through the gate.

"Goodnight, Ehvy," he whispers into the night as he slides his hand into his pocket. "I will see you soon."

His cock twitches again and this time he doesn't fight it as it strains against his pants. *Soon*, he thinks as he returns to the house. For now, his dinner awaits him in the dungeons. And he's fucking starving.

Chapter Eight

EHVY

"...sometime am I all wound with adders who with cloven tongues do hiss me into madness."

The ride back to her apartment in the posh Wraith is quiet as the driver leaves Ehvy to mull over her evening with Will.

The after-touch of his kiss burns on Ehvy's lips and she presses her fingers to her mouth. Her whole body shook at the thought of kissing him, and she was usually not one for initiating that kind of contact. But all the signs were there. How close their bodies were all evening. The way he looked at her. How they held hands. She's a fucking adult, for Christ's sake. Not some teenager groping her way through the world, unsure of who she even is.

Ehvy knows who she is. She's comfortable in her skin. And she knows, without a shadow of a doubt, that she wants Will.

Yet something gnaws at the back of her mind. All the information she gleaned in her search on him points to the historical William Sandridge as being nothing more than a genetic coincidence to the one she spent time with tonight. That is the logical conclusion she must draw from all she found. Because there was nothing unusual about this evening's Will. His skin was a healthy pink, if not on the pale side. His teeth weren't unusually sharp and he drank from the same decanter she had. That was wine, nothing else.

There's no reason to think Will is anything but human. It's not like he could be anything else. What would he be? Something fictional and best left for the pages of a book or a movie screen? Ehvy's seen a lot in life, especially in her career. Nothing that would point to the supernatural. Not without a modicum of doubt, anyway.

Like with the dungeon. Whatever that smell was, Ehvy smelled it in Will's study last week, again at the accident site, and now tonight. Ehvy knows just how powerful the mind can be. Maybe there was *something* in Will's study that smelled good. The lingering scent of his dinner. Now it's what she smells when she thinks of him. The convenience of the situation be damned. She certainly wasn't thinking of him at the site of the accident. At least not initially.

No, because the smell triggered the thought. Not the other way around.

A cackle climbs its way up her tongue, but Ehvy shakes her head and swallows it down.

Ridiculous.

Absolutely ridiculous.

She finds Will attractive and easy to talk to, and she would not kick him out of bed if given the opportunity.

He's not some fictional monster any more than she is developing a blood kink. She has her things, but that's not one of them, despite what her career may say about her.

What none of this explains is why Ehvy had dreamt of him for most of her life. Why she'd been behind Rebecca's eyes in those same dreams. Why the Will of today looks so much like the William of the past, and where she fits into all of this.

The brain is a powerful thing and she can reason away a chance glimpse at their pictures at some point in her life that her mind latched onto. But it's thin and she knows it. The coincidence that Ehvy's desperately trying to convince herself of is tasting more like fate.

Like Will's mouth.

Ehvy sighs into the soft leather of the Wraith's interior and quietly chastises herself. She's being absurd and she'll prove it to herself. He is coming to London this weekend. More time spent with him means more time to find out just what kind of person he is. She'll prove to herself he's just a man. A man who's taken over her mind.

#

Dinner at a private rooftop restaurant overlooking Tower Bridge is an appetizer, just the beginning of a whirlwind courtship. Will fills Ehvy's weeks. He comes to London every few days and shows her sides of the city she's never seen. From the highest-end restaurants to the darkest crypts buried in forgotten places, accessible only with Will's means and connections, it's like London is a whole new place. Foreign, yet familiar at the same time.

It's a side of life Ehvy's never experienced and one that he seems more than willing to share with her. Even better, the more she gets to know him, the more human he becomes. Whatever that scent was doesn't make another appearance, and she watches Will wrap his lips around a fork and consume fine meals like a connoisseur of taste.

Much to her growing frustration, he remains a gentleman, although he gives her glimpses of what's to come. His touches are subtle, but they are worth a thousand words. From a soft kiss on Millennium Bridge to heavier petting buried in a private booth at the back of a darkened restaurant, his hands tentatively wander, graze, and brush against her, teasing frustration into her core. Ehvy's never been one for public displays of affection, but then, she's never met anyone she wants to ride in public. The eyes of the diners make it even more tantalizing.

It's clear from the occasional tent of his pants that he wants what she does, but despite inviting him to her apartment on a number of occasions, and him accepting, he never stays long, claiming an early morning or an off-hours work meeting. Unless he's an amazing actor, there is genuine sorrow in his eyes when he leaves and heady desperation when they pull apart. She's not sure what he's waiting for. She might as well be using fireworks for all the signals she's sending. Her toys are getting mileage, but it's an empty satisfaction.

This celibacy frustrates her. Annoys her, even. But it feels like it's building to something. The more they get to know each other, the deeper their bond grows—the more ravenous they become for each other. The question has been on the tip of her tongue several times, the need to ask why he pushes her away when there's ample opportunity to fuck. But a voice at the back of her mind says, *Wait. Patience.* For this attraction, Ehvy's willing to wait, but her patience is growing thin.

There's so much she knows about him now, none of it supernatural, which she can't help but laugh at. Even when she points out one night over dinner that they only ever see each other in the evening. The one somewhat odd thing about their relationship. The distance, Will says, and the hours they both hold. This is what he can manage, and he wants to manage it for her.

Of course, it makes sense, especially when he comes to London during the week. It's not like she's taking a mountain of time off for him, so she needs to accommodate her schedule as well. It makes perfect sense.

And yet...

She can't shake off the damn notion that he is hiding something. It's annoying her. Will has been nothing but gracious and open, and Ehvy's returned the favor, letting him into her life as much as he's been doing with her. Yet the old images of William Sandridge and Rebecca haunt her. Ehvy's dreams of them haunt her. The waves of déjà vu that wash over her every time she sees Will nearly buckle her knees.

Perhaps this is why she waits. Doesn't push for sex. Some animal instinct telling her there's more to uncover.

Ehvy's growing desire is a specter hovering in the dark, a reminder every time she and Will kiss. Every time their hands touch. When he wraps his arms around her. The way she's drawn to him like an addict with never enough of him to spare. The desperation she feels when he's around, how she wants him inside her, how she wants to be *consumed* by him. It's something she's never felt. Something she's afraid of, for how powerful it feels.

It's like something's been missing from her life, and now she's found it. Never one for believing in the absurd notion that someone else can complete her, Ehvy's always been complete on her own. A concept her friends have trouble understanding. That road went both ways; she could never understand how she could be incomplete without someone else there. Now here's Will, doing something she never thought possible.

Another impossibility beams at her from her phone's screen. An invitation to stay the night at Highcombe Nigh. With Will. This weekend. Heat and cold flush through her body, creating a wave of nausea that spins her stomach. Anxiety and anticipation pulse through her. Ehvy stares at the text as if it's some magical image that will warp if she crosses her eyes hard enough. Or perhaps it'll disappear entirely. A hallucination.

She's been contending with a lot of those lately, especially at Highcombe. Ever since Will started visiting her in London, the feelings of being watched and flickers of images she sees in the streets have disappeared. As if Will's run them off. While at Highcombe, it's like he collects them and stores them within the walls of the manor. The ghosts of the structure's past reach out to her whenever she's in their presence. She's heard too many screams to explain it away as a squeaky door. And that's only in the evening.

What will the house hold for her in the dead of night?

Ehvy exhales, her hand shaking. Right now, the security of her apartment wraps around her. Warm light, comfy rooms, and modern designs give her peace as she sits on the edge of the plush sofa. She can't imagine what it would be like to call a place like Highcombe home.

Ehvy snorts as she thinks of where the television must be, assuming Will even has one. Something so modern seems out of place, even tucked away in a hidden sitting room somewhere in the manor. Will brought her around to all corners of Highcombe, and the rooms looked much like she would expect. Aside from the laptop and cell phone she knows he has, and modern-day basics like electricity and running water, Highcombe is far from modern.

Yet when she thinks of Will, of the two of them together overnight, heat floods her body. Her back against his duvet, his face between her legs, his tongue bringing her to heights she's never experienced. The places his fingers will explore. The feel of his cock as it rams into her.

Ehvy pants as she places her phone on the table, the living room spinning. Her pussy throbs. The desperate need for release is overwhelming. Fucking hell, she's never been this horny in her life. She dashes to her bedroom, clothes flying as she enters, her toys of choice within reach.

She pulls a set of clips from the drawer, a delicate chain stringing them together. Nipples hard and ready, she affixes one clip and then the other, a shudder rolling through her body at the zip of pain. With a little tug on the chain, Ehvy groans, the pain a sweet slice through her core. Her fingers find her cunt and two slide in easily, her body slick and ready. Pain pulses through her breasts in a hum that steadies to a throb of desire.

The need to be filled consumes her as she glances at her nightstand and the thick dildo sitting there. Soon it'll be Will's cock—she fucking hopes. For now, this will do.

Just smaller than her wrist is thick, it would scare some people away, but not Ehvy. A little tug on her chain slicks her more, her body begging for the silicone in her hands. She's not afraid of a little pain. In fact, she welcomes it. Perhaps a reason partners don't stay long. None of them were worthy as far as she's concerned. But Will. Deep down, she knows Will won't run from her desires. He may even hide some darkness of his own.

Her knees on the bed, Ehvy slides the cock in place and settles her entrance at its tip. Slowly, she slides her knees out and allows her pussy to devour the length, taking it centimeter by centimeter. The stretch of her cunt is invigorating, the sharp pierce of pain before it settles into a slick fuck. She imagines Will in the corner, his eyes roving her body as she straddles the toy, his dick in his hand. Ehvy moans as her pussy stretches, taking in more until her body settles, pulsing around the fullness. She grinds against the toy, reveling in her juices slicking it, allowing it to swirl and touch every sensitive place inside her.

Ehvy grabs a breast and pinches the clip, digging it into her nipple and she cries out, grinding harder on the cock. Her hand slides down her body and rubs her clit, pleasure humming through her before she finds the button on the dildo and turns it on. The low hum of the vibration sets her body on fire and her legs spread more, taking the toy as far as it will go.

With her pussy clamped around the toy, Ehvy reaches back to the table and grabs the fluted plug and lube. The thickness of two fingers, she smears the tip in lube before placing it at her tight hole, her body quivering in anticipation. She teases at the opening as the slow rhythm of her body plays with the cock already inside her. Her ass stretches to take the plug. She gasps and moans as she presses, leaning forward to take it deeper. When it seats, she sighs, her body full to the brim and ready to explode.

The slightest brush of her fingers along her stomach has black spots speckling her vision as she rides the fake cock. The image of Will in the corner, stroking himself to the same rhythm, drives her to fuck faster. She reaches around and presses the plug, pulsing it while she rides the cock, her insides practically vibrating to liquid.

A specter of a touch wraps around her throat, and Ehvy throws her head back, giving the phantom more access even if only in her head. She fucks herself, her nipples pulsing painfully, her juices slicking her thighs as the orgasm builds. She wants more, more, more. She needs Will to tear her apart. Devour her.

Her vision goes black as the release presses in. Her breathing stops as her body goes rigid, ecstasy washing through her as she crests the mountain and descends. Ehvy falls back on the bed gasping, her toys still inside her as her pussy pulses. Sweat beads at her hairline, a drop trailing down the back of her neck.

What the hell is Will doing to her? Just the thought of him makes her want to fuck herself all over again.

The haunting scent of sweetness hits her nose and Ehvy's mouth waters, her pussy slick with need all over again. A frown mars her face as she looks to find a small trail of blood on her breast. She unclips the chain and hisses at the bolt of pain, exposing a thin cut on her nipple. A cut that's bleeding.

Ehvy's heart thunders, her hand shaking as she taps a finger into the red and brings it to her nose. A single sniff tells her what she's been afraid of—fresh blood smells divine. A shudder coats her skin and sends shivers through her body as her sweat chills to ice. Not her first time bleeding, but everything seems to have changed since Will came into her life. His presence has flipped a switch in her mind, urging her darkness to come to the forefront.

Taste, a luscious voice says from deep within her mind. *Taste.*

Hesitantly, Ehvy moves her finger to her mouth and allows her tongue to clean the blood from her flesh. Her gums throb with the flavor, her mouth watering for more as ecstasy fills her veins. With the plug still in her ass, her free hand grabs the dildo and pumps yet again, building her wet cunt to another mind-blowing orgasm. She drags her fingers through the blood and laps up every drop before settling into the pillows and allowing the sensations to take her over like a drug.

Rebecca, with hair like moonlight, flashes through her mind as Ehvy plunges the dildo into herself. A wicked smile splays across the phantom's face, baring fangs as blood drips from her tongue. It coats her chin and flows over her breasts as Ehvy fucks herself, moaning into her empty room as Rebecca fills her mind. Glowing wisps of hair turn thick and dark and curly as the images in Ehvy's head shift, and she looks out of different eyes, yet hers all the same. Her body is coated in blood and Will is on his knees at her feet, his mouth buried in her cunt as he devours her and the blood alike. Fangs flash in the ghostly light and Ehvy fucks herself harder, her bedroom wavering in her mind.

A mind that's twisted—fucked up—turned around by a man that's blown into her life like a gale and swept her along with it. New kinks, new desires, an overwhelming need to get fucked. Phantom Will's fangs bite into her thigh, the imagined pain slicking the toy cock she drives into her body.

She wants him. Fucking wants him like no other. Yet he feels like a monster coming out of the woods ready to devour her, body and soul. And she wants nothing more than to get on her knees before him and offer herself as a sacrifice.

Who the fuck thinks like this?

She does.

What the fuck is wrong with her?

Ehvy can wonder all she wants, but she knows the answer. Will. Will is what's wrong with her. And what's right with her. It's just her head twisting him into something inhuman, but even that image doesn't dissuade her. In fact, it does the opposite. As another orgasm builds, Ehvy can't help but question the things he does to her mind and why she wants more of it.

So much more.

Thoughts of a forever young Will, of a violent history of Highcombe, of blood-sucking monsters flow through Ehvy's mind as her body explodes with pleasure. Her back arches as she throbs, gasps filling her ears as she comes down for a second time with thoughts of Will beside her. On her. Filling her up and making her question everything she thinks she knows about herself.

Ehvy fears the darkness Will is bringing out in her, yet she quivers with the anticipation of it.

She breathes into her pillow and smiles, the sweet metal of blood tickling her tongue as she thinks of Will and what's to come.

Chapter Nine

WILL

*"...thy groans did make wolves howl and penetrate
the breasts of ever angry bears: it was a torment
to lay upon the damned..."*

The hunt is usually the most fun he can have, but lately, it's a chore half-heartedly performed after he finishes with Ehvy for the evening. It's a means to an end. A way to pass the time until he can see her again.

Will lopes after his latest mark as the man runs into the tree line, screaming and panting for all the world to hear. Humans are no match for him, though. It's darling how they try. Between him and the sorcery the witch works to dull minds and memories, these breathing flesh suits don't stand a chance.

Using his vampiric speed would take what little fun he's having out of the chase right now, so Will allows his prey to gain some distance before finishing the game. Flashes of shimmering white-blonde hair flicker through the trees as Will runs, and his heart swells with thoughts of Rebecca. When those tresses morph into dark, wild curls reaching to him like vines to a trellis, it's his cock that swells. Hunger roars in his chest and his fangs descend, ready to tear into his dinner. His mark squirms something fierce until Will knocks him unconscious, a harsh blow that cracks the man's skull. No matter. He won't live to see the dawn.

Longing thrums through him as he drags the man into the dungeon, thinking of Ehvy and the things they will do together. A laugh layered with voices haunts his mind and his pulse quickens. At long last, she has agreed to stay the night with him. Oh, how he wanted to demolish her any number of times they had been together, public or private, but he held fast. Waiting for her to be ready. *Truly* ready. He thinks she is.

Finally.

Not only in the way she looks at him, her lips glistening and full, pouting and waiting for his bite, but how she clings to him. Her hands wrapped in his with her body pressed against him. He can feel it. The way her eyes dilate when he knows fresh blood is near, and how her nose tilts into the air to inhale it.

Rebecca's memory haunts Ehvy's human form. Her essence surrounds the mortal woman, but the more time he spends with the captivating human, the more Rebecca fades between them. Will holds the image of Rebecca in his mind while he looks for hints of his beloved in this new woman less and less. Ehvy is her own being with some ingredients from his dead lover. She is far from the whole recipe, yet just as enticing.

Wrists and feet in manacles, clothes in tatters and barely covering the whimpering man, Will's victim hangs suspended over the stone floor in the dungeon with the drain under his feet. He is barely conscious, but when Will's nail slices along his stomach, the man's eyes flutter and a moan escapes his lips.

Will's fangs descend, his gums aching as he takes two fingers and slides them into the slit. Warmth and wetness of the man's body envelop his hand as visions of Ehvy flicker through his mind.

She lies before him; her legs spread wide as she fucks herself, putting on a show just for him. Teasing him. Will is ready to fall to his knees to beg for just a sliver of her body. His eyes roll into the back of his head as he unbuckles his belt and unbuttons his pants, freeing his solid cock from its confines.

His whole fist enters the man's abdomen, his fingers wrapping around whatever he can grab as he strokes himself with his free hand. Each slide builds the pleasure at the center of him, the ringing in his ears growing as he opens his mouth and groans.

Sobs from the hanging, mutilated man break Will's concentration and he snarls, his cock painfully hard as anger boils his blood. He rips his hand from inside the man and grabs his victim's face before slicing each cheek clean through with a talon-like nail. The man's jaw hangs open as tears flow down his mangled face; Will buries his bloody fist in the man's mouth. Gags fill the small stone room as he drags his finger through the man's tongue and rips it from his head.

The thick, meaty appendage flops in his hand, still warm and wet, and Will smiles as he presses it to his cock and continues to stroke. He plunges his other hand back into the man. Strangled gurgles bubble from the ripped-open face as Will continues to fuck himself until his moans choke him. He throws his head back and erupts at the man's feet, dowsing his victim's shoes in his cum.

Will gasps through the final throes of his orgasm and lets the man's tongue splat to the floor before he licks the blood from one hand, then the other. With his cock still out, he's at his victim's throat in a flash, his movement like lightning. Flesh snaps and blood pours down his throat as he drinks his fill, satisfying himself for the time being.

He cleans up with a nearby rag and dresses, reminding himself to tidy up later. Will tosses the rag in his mess and smiles, not seeing the corpse in front of him. His eyes, his mind, and his body are only for Ehvy.

#

Will shouldn't be nervous like some child expecting a present, but he is. Ehvy will arrive at any moment, bag in hand, ready to climb into his bed. Giddiness flutters in his chest and he curses himself for the feeling, foreign though it is. Killing brings him joy, sure enough, and there's plenty in the world worth living for. But Ehvy—like Rebecca—brings him such a savage life that it's overwhelming. He's so close to having her for himself, transforming her into what she's meant to be.

Ehvy's train arrived half an hour ago. Only minutes left.

The village surrounding Highcombe Nigh is a humble one and Will wants the dinner to be special, not mired in the dark pits of some dingy pub. So, he unearthed wine from the cellars and had his chef cook the finest Michelin-worthy meal. It won't be about being full, but about being lavished.

He will lavish her.

The sound of a car door closing echoes through the manor, his hyper-sensitive ears picking up the noise from his study. He jolts from his chair, nearly toppling it, and straightens his jacket. She asked him once why he always dressed up and he had to hide his sneer at the casual styles worn by men today. How slovenly they look. Instead, he told her that since his suits are bespoke, they are far more comfortable than stiff denim could ever be.

Besides, a suit looks so much better. Perhaps it's his ancient blood roaring through his veins, but Will enjoys looking finely pressed, and he will enjoy spoiling Ehvy in his finery. She dresses well enough now, but with him, it will be only the finest. It's what they deserve.

A member of the staff beats him to the door, and he waves the man away before running his hand through his hair and checking his reflection in a nearby mirror. A myth, he learned long ago, that vampires cannot see their reflections. He adjusts his jacket once more and sets his hand on the door handle.

She's not looking at him, but down, watching her feet make each step. She almost looks worried, her brow creased, a small frown pulling down over her brilliant eyes. Yet when she looks at him, whatever indecision she was warring with disappears, pushed away by a beaming smile and a gasp of a breath as she rests her gaze on him.

"Darling," he says as she whispers, "Will." He reaches out, beckoning her into his embrace.

Ehvy places her hand in his and he pulls her to him, the overnight bag on her shoulder forgotten as she melts into the curve of his body. His arms wrap around her back as he lowers his lips to hers. The world around them disappears. All that remains is the heat of her flesh, the slick moistness of her lips, her tongue teasing his teeth, and her body pressing against his cock.

The animal in him wants to say "fuck dinner" and take her in the foyer. Rip her clothes off and rut like dogs. Based on the little moan in her throat, she'd welcome it. But he's determined to make this a good night. A night she will remember for the rest of her long, long life.

The evening starts with a five-course dinner that won't fill her, despite the number of plates on offer. A sloshing stomach won't do on his little human. When they're done, they don their jackets for an evening stroll around the property. It's Will's way to allow a chill to settle into her bones before bringing her inside for drinks by the fire to warm up and loosen their limbs. Ehvy still seems stiff, her shoulders tenser than they should be. Perhaps it's what they will do, the anticipation of that initial fuck. How adorable. She must be nervous. For good reason.

When their conversation lulls, weight appears to settle behind her eyes and her shoulders sag. He's not even sure if Ehvy knows how her body has shifted, but he sees it. Worry flits in her gaze and her head tilts the slightest bit as she appears to mull something over.

RIAN ADARA

"What is it?" he asks, his brows furrowing. She shakes her head and waves him off, but he won't accept that. "No, something's troubling you. Please tell me." His tone sounds like begging to his ears, and he hides a wince, keeping his gaze trained on her.

"No, it's stupid. Absurd, really. It's nothing. I'm just—I'm being silly," Ehvy responds, trying to smile through her quivering lips.

Will sets his tumbler on a nearby table and pulls himself from the chair to kneel in front of her. He places his hands on her thighs, the heat of her pulsing through the fabric as he gazes into her eyes.

"Please don't say that. You're not silly. There's so much we still don't know about each other, and I want to lay my soul at your feet. You must never be afraid of asking me anything." His hands squeeze her legs, a reassuring pressure as she shudders with a sigh. "Please don't be afraid of me."

It's not what he means to say, but it's what comes out of his mouth. It's more of a plea than he cares for. Will lets the words lie as Ehvy's gaze roams over his face. He slides his hands up her legs, feeling her heartbeat pick up. She traces a finger along his forehead and down his jaw before pressing her finger into his lower lip.

"You're changing me, Will. It's not you who I'm afraid of, but myself," she whispers as she leans down, her knees spreading, and presses her lips to his.

He slides between her legs, fitting himself there like it's a place he's never left. His hands move to her hips before he pulls her closer. She frames his body in hers, her thighs squeezing around him, and he leans in. Ehvy runs her fingers through his hair as she pulls his head closer, her tongue probing his mouth as he fights to keep his desire in check.

Her skin is silk to the touch, her lips plush like velvet as he runs his hands up her back. She arches into him, pushing her breasts into his chest as she moans. His cock twitches at the sound, the heat pulsing off her, the smell of her taking him over.

Everything in him screams to rush her upstairs, but now is not the time to scare her, and speeds like that would send her running. No. There are steps to take. *Taking* Ehvy is only the first step.

Ankles knot behind his back as she pulls herself closer and Will stands with her latched to him, hanging onto him like he is life itself. His hand finds her ass, lush and thick, and squeezes, eliciting a gasp from her precious mouth. Her teeth bite into his lip and pull, nips that shoot lightning into his depths. Teeth trace his jaw and nibble on the flesh of his neck, his earlobe, and his cock hardens despite his best effort. A growl rumbles low in his chest and Ehvy presses herself into him.

"Perhaps we should get to bed," he whispers as her tongue teases at the crux of his shoulder. She nips him as he sucks in a breath.

"I think we should," she says with a smile that spreads against his skin as her mouth makes its way back to his.

She unlocks her ankles and Will places her on her feet before leading her out of the sitting room. They travel back through the center of the house, up the grand staircase, and to his bedroom toward the back.

Stepping into his room must be overwhelming, and he tries to look at it through her eyes. Rich mahogany, deep burgundy, and midnight black fill the space, with an intricately carved headboard centered on a four-poster bed. To most, it screams, *Get away*. But Ehvy moves farther into the room. It's old-world and Gothic. The lights are kept low, with candles scattered throughout, but also the modern world's electricity is found in lamps and a digital clock on a bedside table.

Will does not dwell in the past, but he has his comforts. Now he will share them with Ehvy.

Her things are already here, tucked into a corner, but as he turns, that's not what she's looking for. She only has eyes for him, and he is right there to absorb her light. Her arms wrap around his neck and he lifts her from the floor, walking her to the foot of the massive bed. Will sets her on the edge and slips her shoes from her feet while keeping his gaze on her face.

"Tell me what you like, love," he whispers into her mouth. "I long to make you scream."

She can't know how badly he wants to hear her wail.

Ehvy slides her hands into his jacket, pushing it off his shoulders and down his arms as he lets it fall to the floor. She hooks her heels around his knees as she unbuttons his shirt, biting her lip as she smiles at him.

"You're going to have to work for that," she says in a husky whisper. "I'm not just going to give you my secrets. There's no fun in that."

Will growls as he presses his lips to hers and moves his hands under her blouse. The warmth of her nearly buckles his knees, but he lifts her shirt off, leaving her in her bra and he in an unbuttoned Oxford standing between the legs of the woman he's addicted to.

"We have time enough yet for me to peel away your layers and devour the sweet fruit that lies beneath." The tip of his tongue flicks at her lips and she shudders under his touch. With one hand, he unclasps her bra and it falls away, exposing hardened nipples and breasts waiting for his mouth. "There goes one already."

"What do you like?" she pants as Will grazes a finger down her chest, swirling it around her nipple before moving it down her side.

A smile pulls at the corners of his lips, and he can't help but tease, "I don't think you're ready for that."

There's a tug at his waist as his belt buckle jingles and his pants loosen. "I'm here, aren't I?" The sound of the zipper echoes loudly in the expansive bedroom, and the shush of his pants falling to his ankles is like a boulder crashing from a cliff. "Besides, you'd be surprised what I'm ready for."

Despite how ready Will knows she is, he's still apprehensive. It could all go wrong. It could be too much, and he doesn't want to think about what comes after that. Ehvy living would be a threat to him because of how much she would know; his influence, and the witch's, can only go so far. He hopes it doesn't come to that. He hopes she accepts him the way he thinks she will.

"Let's find out," Will whispers just over her mouth as he presses his fingers between her breasts and pushes her onto the bed. She moves toward the pillows, but he grabs her knees to keep her in place. "Stay there," he tells her with a wicked grin.

A confused look passes over her face as she watches him remove the rest of his clothing, his taut body and throbbing cock on full display. Ehvy's gaze roves over him, across the planes of his chest and down the light trail of hair on his stomach, looking at him with such longing that Will is almost tempted to thrust into her right now.

Almost.

Instead, he peels her clothing away, removing her pants leg by leg, leaving kisses at her ankle, her knee, at the inner thickness of her thigh. All that stands between him and her luscious core is a thin pair of lace underwear. Black like her bra. She wore a matching set for him. He smiles at the thought and presses his nose into her sheathed slit before running his tongue up her sensitive mound.

Will leans over her, one hand massaging her thigh as she pants under him. The other crooks a finger in the band of the small scrap of material and drags it down her legs. Instead of standing back up, he remains on his knees, the height of the bed placing her at his shoulders. The perfect height for him to feast.

He grabs her thighs and yanks her closer, eliciting a gasp from her as she grips onto the duvet for support.

"Don't worry, love. I won't let you fall," he says as he presses into her thighs, spreading her wide open for him.

One arm wraps around her leg, and he presses his cheek into the warm flesh, nuzzling her. Kissing her. Nipping at her skin. Lower. Lower. His tongue teases at her opening, circling her core as choking gasps erupt from Ehvy's mouth. The tip of his tongue teases her entrance before sliding in, probing her. Lapping her up as he plunges into her. Her body writhes against his face, her hand fisting his hair and pulling him closer.

He pulls his tongue out and laps up, licking at her lips before circling her clit. Slow, steady waves of his tongue pulse against her most sensitive spot before his mouth latches on and he sucks. Ehvy's back arches, pressing her pussy into his face. He presses in harder, sucking and licking her to her peak.

But he pulls away before she can crest, blowing on her moist cunt as it swells with blood for him. Knowing what she likes isn't a guess. She is not Rebecca, yet she is in so many ways. Starting with what Rebecca liked is easy enough.

He turns his head and focuses on her folds, running his tongue along the sensitive skin before he grazes a fang across the flesh. Ehvy inhales sharply as blood wells in the thin cut, but it doesn't last long. Will presses his tongue to the wound, running it along the slit within her slit. He takes her lip in his mouth and sucks, drawing out more blood, as much as he can without her noticing, but she doesn't seem to care.

Moans collect in her throat, her head thrown back, one hand fisting the duvet as he eats her whole.

Her cries echo through the room as her body stiffens. Will dives further into her cunt, lapping her up, swirling and flicking his way through her body in ways that make her pant. Until her body freezes and a wailing cry erupts from her mouth. He continues licking, teasing at her entrance, flicking her clit as her body jerks, the orgasm waning.

Her juices coat his mouth, and he wipes it away before he crawls up her body, his tongue teasing along her flesh, licking a rib, flicking a nipple before he settles himself on top of her, his cock between her legs and his lips on hers. Ehvy drinks him in, pulling his head as close to her as she can get as she snakes her fingers through his hair. Her taste is divine, an elixir he will drink for eternity if she'll let him.

She reaches for him as he pulls away and he whispers into her mouth, "That's just the beginning, my love."

With a hand under her back, he rolls them over so Ehvy is on top. She straddles his lap, his length resting against her as she grinds into it, her body begging him. *Not yet*, he thinks. *There's still more to do.*

Will's fingers toy with her lips as her tongue emerges to flick their tips. He drags his fingers down her mouth, her chin, the center of her chest before he grazes a breast and grabs a nipple. He circles the sensitive skin before his thumb and forefinger grip onto her nipple and tug. His gaze finds her face, but her eyes are closed as she revels in the sensation.

"Look at me." His voice is breathy as Ehvy's eyes flutter open and lock onto his.

He pinches her nipple harder and twists as she sucks air between her teeth. Taking it as a sign, he lets go and Ehvy hisses again.

"Don't stop." Her head shakes as her thumb grazes his mouth. She dips down and brushes her lips against his. When he reaches for a kiss he craves, she pulls away, a sinister smile on her face. "Harder."

There is more of Rebecca in her than he imagined.

He finds her nipple again, Ehvy's eyes steady on him, and he pinches, tugs, twists. Ehvy grinds against him until her fingers find their way to her pussy. Like lightning, he snatches her hand away and a cry dies in her throat, a pitiful pout on her face.

"You're mean," she pants as her hips move against his length.

"This isn't mean, love. But perhaps this is."

With one breast still in his grip, he dips his head to the

other and takes it in his mouth, teeth clenching around the nipple as he sucks. His tongue laps at the sensitive skin underneath before he tugs on the nipple with his teeth while his fingers occupy the other.

A warm hand lands on his shoulders as Ehvy steadies herself and grinds her way to release while Will works her body. Until he stops. The move is so sudden it takes her a second to realize her pleasure has stopped. When she does, she frowns at him. Her juices soak his cock, and he longs to plunge it deep within her.

"Say you trust me, Ehvy," Will says as he cups her face in his hands.

"I wouldn't be here if I didn't," she tells him as she plants a feather-light kiss on his lips.

"Say it," he demands, wanting to hear those words fall from her lips before he does what he wants to do.

With no hesitation, Ehvy says, "I trust you."

A smile spreads across his face as he reaches toward the settee at the end of the bed. Cold metal meets his hand and when he pulls it back, Ehvy's eyes go wide, fear trickling in at the sight of the small blade in his hand. Though it is little more than a letter opener, he can understand the stiffness of her body and the way her hand clenches on his shoulder. All the while his cock pulses with need from the anticipation of what he's about to do.

"Perhaps now I can show you what I like," Will says as he settles the blade in his hand. It's clear she likes pain. But how much?

"And what is that?" she asks, her voice raspy. He's sure he can hear curiosity in her tone, tinged with a hint of fear.

Slowly. He must move slowly.

"Is it cutting?" she asks when he takes too long to respond.

Her eyes rove over his body, looking for marks and finding none. Not that any would stay on his flesh for long.

Will shakes his head. "Close, but not quite."

Before he can say it, her wet lips form the word. "Blood."

There's a quiver to her lower lip and for a moment her gaze goes vacant, as if a memory sifts to the forefront of her mind. It's there and gone in a second before she focuses on his face. Will's small smile says it all.

"May I show you? The pain will be little more than a flash. The blade is quite sharp," he says as candlelight glints off the silver.

Ehvy's stillness has worry settling into his stomach, but after an interminably long moment, she nods, a smile flickering on her lips. "If you hadn't noticed, I don't mind pain."

Her heartbeat is like a hummingbird's, wild and anxious in her chest, but what she's presenting to him is calm. Blood thrums through her veins, keeping her heart beating, and he knows this is what she wants. Apprehension still lingers in her eyes, but she is willing.

"Pain, yes," Will says as his tongue flicks her nipple before he looks at her. "But I long to taste you. Your lifeblood in my mouth. Will you allow me to taste you?"

His cock twitches at his request and Ehvy gasps. Her eyes are heavily lidded, her pupils dilated as she considers him. He's already had a taste, of course. One he took. Just a hint. But now he wants more and he doesn't want to take it without this fine specimen's permission.

Another long moment pulses between them before a shaky breath flows over her lips and she nods.

There and gone in a flash, Will slashes the blade up under her breast, creating a thin line that reaches her nipple, blood pooling in the cut within moments. A delayed gasp tumbles out of her mouth, and she digs her fingers into his shoulder again as he bends to her breast. Her pussy rubs against his shaft, damp and eager as his mouth latches onto her, his tongue lapping at the sliver of blood.

Will suckles her, his teeth aching to bite, tear in, and guzzle more blood, but he holds himself back as he draws from the minuscule well he's created. Ehvy's hands climb the back of his neck and hold his head to her. When he looks up, her head is thrown back, her body pressing into him as he draws blood from a wound that's far too small for his liking. But he must take it slowly. She's receptive. It's only a matter of time.

She slumps over, panting, a moan low in her throat. Her eyes trail up his body and when they land on his face, there's fire in her gaze, ready to ignite him.

The remnants of Rebecca linger in Ehvy's eyes, but it's this modern woman on top of him who captivates him. Who swirls his mind into a cyclone of desire and emotion that he hasn't known in a hundred years.

Her gaze bores into his soul like she's etching the lines of his face into her memory. The blade flashes before he realizes it's in her hand, and her knees spread wider as she settles herself onto him.

The delicate touch of her hand finds his fingers and she lifts them, the blade point ready. She looks at him with her lips parted as she waits before saying, "May I?"

Anxious desire pulses through his cock at her question, the need to plunge into her depths overwhelming. Yet Will manages to control himself and provide her with a consenting nod.

The silver quivers as she presses the point into his fingertip. Her eyes glance up and Will looks at her with a small smile on his face. Encouraging. Enabling. Demanding.

The snick of punctured flesh sounds like a thunderbolt as Ehvy presses the knife in and drags, awkward with the blade. The cut is deeper than what he made on her, but no matter. It'll be gone soon enough, anyway. But not before blood beads in the cut; her eyes flutter as the scent hits her nose.

Another battle of the war she wages inside herself shifts across her face as she stares at the blood. Ehvy is an open book to him right now. He doesn't need mind-reading powers to know that she knows she shouldn't want this. She shouldn't respond to blood like she is. She shouldn't be here with him, playing with knives. Yet she fights every instinctual inclination that rises within her, determined to remain spread across his cock, playing with his blood.

Just how he wants her.

Still, she hesitates and Will takes it upon himself to brush her fingers from his hand and move to her lip where he hovers the blood just out of reach. Her nostrils flare and her slick cunt grinds against his length as she struggles with herself. When he turns the pad of his finger around and presses the blood to her lip, Ehvy freezes, allowing the blood to bead there before her tongue reaches out and tastes him on her lips.

A shudder rumbles through her at the single drop. The blood alone—and vampire blood at that—is like the finest drug to a human. A drug that will kill her if consumed in too high a quantity. So Will must be careful. His shaft presses into her opening as she licks more of his blood from her lips before grabbing his finger and burying it in her mouth. Her tongue swirls around the pad, probing into the cut to draw out more blood.

Oh, my love. Soon.

Will bites through his lip, drawing blood, then grabs Ehvy by the jaw just hard enough to get her attention and takes her lip in his. A tiny cry blows across his face when he bites down, drawing her blood and crashing into her. Their mouths tangle with the kiss, the blood slick between them. So much of her is on his face, her heady scent filling him. She draws on his lip, sucks on it, trying to get more of him before he wraps his arms around her and flips her onto her back.

Ehvy gasps, but he doesn't give her a moment to think. With his cock in hand, he presses it to her opening and slides in, her tight cunt expanding around him. Blood smears her chin as she sticks her fingers in his mouth, sliding them along his tongue and down his throat as he pushes deeper into her. She spreads her legs for him and Will presses one of her knees to the bed as he buries himself inside her.

"Fuck me," she whispers. "Hard."

He needn't be told twice.

He starts slow, reveling in the feel of her sliding on and off him. Ehvy's hands move to his ass, pushing him, guiding him. He picks up the tempo, driving in harder the more she moans. Cries. Screams as his cock hits the hilt and she can't spread her legs wide enough.

Will lowers himself over her, his hair brushing her face, his hand at the side of her head as their eyes lock on each other.

"I don't want to break you, dear one," Will says with a smile as his tongue flicks her lips.

Ehvy smiles back, lust heavy in her eyes as she tilts her chin up. "Let me decide that for myself."

She hooks an ankle over his leg and collapses his arm before rolling them over and mounting him. Will's head spins and he can't help but laugh as she takes control, using him like a toy to be fucked. Ehvy's actions, her demands, the power hiding in such a small body, throb through him, his cock aching as her pussy sheathes it.

He's fully seated as Ehvy grinds her hips on him, rolling and waving as she finds a rhythm, getting his cock to hit a particular spot. The vision on top of him is worthy of sonnets, a painting the size of the estate itself, and corpses piled to the rafters. With both hands, he plays with her breasts, twisting and pulling her nipples as she writhes, fucking him the way she demands to be fucked, her delicious cunt warm and tight around him.

But Will's control is slipping through his fingers. In a move he may regret later, he sits up, wraps his hand around her throat, and pins her to the nearby post. Her legs wrap around him as he kneels on the bed. The movement takes little more than a second, faster than Ehvy can process, and by then he's already pumping into her, thrusting harder and faster as he slides his hands down her arms and pushes them over her head.

He holds them there as he rams into her, her hips meeting every thrust, her back arching to press her breasts into him. They're just close enough for him to take one in his mouth and bite, hard enough to draw blood. Ehvy doesn't register it, lost in the feel of his cock moving inside her. He laps at the blood, sucking and pulling her nipple, before he finds her mouth again and captures her in another deep kiss.

Her heartbeat escalates as her body builds to its zenith. Ehvy twitches as the orgasm grows and she loses the control she's trying to maintain.

"Look at me when you come," Will says, his voice hoarse.

Ehvy struggles to open her eyes, the pleasure overwhelming her, and stares into his. He grips her hands over her head as he drives into her, their bodies barreling together as Ehvy's moans grow.

"I'm going to come," she gasps. "I'm...I'm..."

She throws her head back and cries out as her pussy pulses around him and he drives deeper into her. Harder. More fervently. Drawing out her pleasure as much as he can until his orgasm overtakes him. He spills into her as his body shakes, her legs clenching around him as if she's afraid he'll let go. Will slumps into her, her sweaty skin a balm against him as her arms fall and wrap around his shoulders.

He has fucked plenty in his long life, but it's been too long since he's had something like this. An earth-shattering, mind-numbing fuck.

It's only the beginning.

He wraps his arms around her and holds her close, her heavy breathing a cool breeze across his back as he lowers them both to the bed. They lie there, on their sides, legs tangled together. His cock slips free and she seems unbothered by the mess he spills. She runs her fingers through his hair, brushing it from his face, before sliding her nail along his jaw.

There's still blood caked on her lips and chin, but she pays it no mind as she gazes at him as if there's nothing else in the world. As he looks at her, this room, the manor, the emptiness of these last hundred years, disappears. Ehvy is everything he thought she would be.

He's going to enjoy bringing her into this new life.

Chapter Ten

EHVY

"Good wombs have borne bad sons..."

A bib of dried blood coats her breasts, pieces flaking onto the counter every time she moves. A muted pink stains her lips and chin and smears her cheeks. Ehvy's hair sits piled on top of her head as she runs water over her chest and face, sloughing her and Will's blood away. Under the soft light of the massive bathroom, a room that's almost as big as her entire apartment, she can convince herself she's still human. Yet something feels like it's shifted inside of her, something dark and brooding crawling from the shadows and sniffing its way into the light. More so now than ever before.

She has no idea what time it is. Late. It feels like something's wrong with her, like her engine won't stop revving even though she's already taken her foot off the accelerator. She's never had the desire to fuck more than once in a single night, but with Will, it's been three times so far. She's exhausted, yet her pussy throbs at the thought of him. The low pulse of well-earned pain between her legs tells her to take a break even as it begs for more.

Ehvy's head spins with the revelations of the evening, information Will can't know she gathered about him. Dots she's connecting she thought for sure couldn't connect because fiction is for books and movies—not real life.

She reaches for a nearby silk nightdress and pulls on a matching robe, a gift from Will that glides across her skin. Little impressions of teeth dot her shoulder, and her breasts ache from his bites. A small bruise blooms on her neck, near her ear, and the taste of blood lingers on her lips.

When she blinks, the lights flicker and something flashes in the mirror. Something blonde and thin, pale as the dead, with a wicked look of joy on her face. But the vision disappears in a flash, leaving Ehvy breathing hard. She switches the light off and exits the bathroom, but she doesn't go back to bed. Will's deep breathing prompted her to get up in the first place; with the silence hanging in the room, she takes it as her opportunity to explore.

The tubal she had three years ago negates any worry she may have about pregnancy. The blood concerns her, though. Less for the risks it poses, since they cleared that question weeks ago, and more for what it does to her. How overwhelming the smell of it is. How luxurious the taste. What it does to her body. Ehvy is nothing but human. Of that, she is sure. But Will is changing her. She has no doubt about that. In impossible ways.

Pain has always been a kink she enjoyed, but it turned off her partners. Not Will. He leans into it, teasing her with the knife blade, drawing blood, drinking from her and she from him. Blood never did it for her, but just the thought of Will's blood dampens her apex. Her aching nipples pulse. Between his teeth and his hands, she's not sure how much more her body can handle in a single night.

Lit by the ambient light of the digital clock, an anachronistic thing in this decadent room, Ehvy tiptoes to the door and lets herself out through the smallest crack she can make. She needs to check out the library.

In most other houses, hallways would be dark at night. But as she makes her way downstairs, soft light illuminates her path. Images of a potential past move through her mind —how dark these halls used to be when electricity didn't exist and burning candles all night wasn't feasible. Heavy darkness sits crowded in the corners and under the stairs. She can only imagine what the rest of the house would look like if that darkness was set free.

When she stands in front of the library door, her hand on the doorknob, she turns it and stops when an idea comes to her. Perhaps what she's looking for isn't the library. It's too open. Too exposed. Too close to the tour route.

No, it's not the library she should search to find his secrets. It's the study.

Will's study.

The one they first met in. The one he said no one could see. If secrets are going to be stored somewhere, that would be a better place to start.

The manor is quiet as she tiptoes her way to the forbidden room, peeks of wooden floor around the runners chilling her toes as she moves, her silken robe fluttering behind her.

She passes the hall where Rebecca's portrait hangs, and

the urge to look at it again comes over her. Standing at the entrance to the corridor, Ehvy can see the edges of the frame and pieces of the dress the woman is wearing in it. Hair, pale and shimmering even in oil paint, flutters off the canvas in an unseen breeze, reaching into the manor. Strands sparkling like cobwebs. The world blurs as the painting shimmers. Fingertips wrap over the gilt frame. More hair flies out, the slope of a nose, one blinking eye. The lights flicker and it's once again just a corridor.

With a hard swallow, Ehvy shakes her head and continues on, not giving it a second look. She doesn't want to waste time; she doesn't know how long Will will stay asleep, and she doesn't want to press her luck. Should he wake and find her gone, she has several excuses ready to explain why she isn't in bed, but she'd rather not use them. Despite everything, Ehvy wants to crawl back into bed with him and feel his warm flesh against hers, his lips on her skin. His cock in her yet again.

Her pussy throbs at the thought, an ache buried deep in her core sending need across her skin. Will is like a drug, a thing she craves. She thought it was bad when their relationship was more innocent—little more than kisses and wandering hands. Now it doesn't feel like she can get enough of him; what she gets isn't even scratching the surface of her desire.

Will's study is dark, with no windows to even offer ambient light. Luckily, there's enough light from the corridor for Ehvy to feel her way around the walls and flick a nearby switch. The corner lamp washes the room in a muted glow as she walks in. What she's looking for likely isn't in a stack of papers on his desk or buried in a drawer. A family history like what she wants to see might be in a folder. Or in an old book hidden on a shelf.

Books line one whole side of the study and Ehvy scans the spines, looking for anything that may stand out. A few books are unmarked, but when she pulls them out, they're just old ledgers, some dating back hundreds of years. She's not looking for a secret diary where someone spilled all the Sandridge family's dirty details. An old photo album, maybe. Or a genealogy guide.

Something to prove Will is human, not an ancient immortal creature.

In the back corner of the study, on a shelf over her head but not out of reach, sits a battered black leather-bound tome that begs Ehvy to touch it. However, the call of the room beyond the study is louder. It captured her attention the first time she was here. The expansive darkness within calls to her like the scent that drew her to Will.

A scent she now knows is fresh blood. There was fresh blood in that room the day she met Will. A lot, if the ease with which she found it was any sign. Like at the accident outside King's Cross, or worse. The thought of what that could mean ripples through Ehvy's mind, fangs, and blood and moans filling her head before she shakes it all away.

Instead, she reaches for the book. Cracked leather presses into her skin as she pulls it from the shelf and flips through the pages.

The inside cover is a vast family tree going back hundreds of years. The Sandridge line is expansive, most of the branches reaching deep into the bottom of the page. A few in the middle stop short. Children dying young, perhaps. Or someone choosing not to procreate, however odd that was back then. One in particular draws her attention, hanging on the edge of the page and stopping short with a single name: William Sandridge.

Father, Charles, and mother, Katherine. There are four siblings here, all with lines that carry on. But William's stops. Judging by where it stops, it was a long time ago.

A shuddering breath flows across her lips as she stares at Will's familial history. This wouldn't be odd if it were any other name. But it's Will's. William Sandridge from an eon ago. Nine hundred years, maybe? There's a William in the early 20th century based on the photos she found. And there's a William now who looks a hell of a lot like the 1920s William. But the family tree bears no other William in any line except this one.

Ehvy turns the ancient pages, the barely legible scrawl limiting what she could read. The clock is ticking. Toward the back, she assumes when photography became more common, photos litter the pages. There's a portrait of a dour-looking man on a piece of metal. Then there are photographs backed with thick cardboard. People from history she doesn't recognize—and two she does.

Rebecca is in these photos going back to the 1800s, based on the type of photo and the dress. Same with Will. Their clothes change, as does their hair. But their faces stay the same. Ehvy's seen a hundred and fifty years of photographs and Will's and Rebecca's faces are the same in all of them.

She can hear the coincidences flying out the window.

No. None of this is coincidence or some genetic fluke or anything she can explain away.

The book closes with a resounding thud, and Ehvy stills,

listening for the sound of someone approaching. The house remains silent in the late night. She slides the book back onto the shelf and the secret room, bathed in black, calls her attention once more.

She should go back to Will before she's missed. She doesn't want him to find her snooping. Except that room is like a hook in her middle, dragging her closer. Her gut tells her to leave it be, but her feet are already walking her toward the darkness.

It presses on her like a void as she steps up to a black so dark she might cease to exist if she steps into it. A switch sits just on the inside of the room and she flicks it. Not sure what she expects, she's still disappointed to find no proper answers.

The room is more spartan than the study. An old medical room, perhaps. There's a small plain desk in the corner, a vast difference from the mahogany monolith in the study. Rickety wooden tables dot the room and hover over floor drains, some draped in cloth.

She walks up to the closest table and runs her fingers along the old wood, half expecting it to tell her its secrets. Other than the slight tinge of antiseptic reminding her of her lab, there's nothing to this room at all.

It is clear that it's a room that is used, and the thought churns her stomach. If it weren't, there'd be dust coating the tables and desk covering the floor like in the ballroom. Or protective sheets would cover everything. The room is old, but not left to seed. A closed-up room is just that: a closed room. This room is not closed. Not at all.

What could Will use a room like this for?

Something prickles along Ehvy's spine and she turns,

gasping. Will's tall form fills the doorway. He rests lazily on the frame, his ankles crossed, silk pajama bottoms hugging his hips while his torso remains bare. His pale, lean, muscled frame in full view.

He cocks his head and one corner of his mouth quirks. "What are you doing, love?"

Ehvy's heart thunders and heat rushes to her face. Guilt swells within her and she grasps for an excuse, some justifiable reason for her to be there. One of the many she had prepared. Until the desire to *know* overwhelms her. The desire for truth. If he's merely a man with a particular set of kinks, then they can laugh about this. Ehvy can stew in the awkwardness for a while and they can get back to it. The other option...is impossible.

Yet...

She gathers herself and pulls her shoulders back, keeping her eyes on Will. "Searching. I was searching."

A flirtatious frown settles across his face. "Searching for what, then?"

At first, she can't say it. Her response stalls on her tongue, the words afraid to move the rest of the way out. Like she's done so many times over these weeks, she pushes her fear aside and moves forward. Toward Will.

"Answers," she says, little more than a gasp.

She curses herself for how weak it sounds, yet the way he looks at her doesn't speak to that weakness. It speaks to intrigue and something else. Excitement, maybe?

"And what answers would those be, darling?" he asks as he closes the distance between them. "I told you, I'm yours to peel open and explore. All you need to do is ask."

The smell of him overwhelms her even from halfway

across the room. The heady scent of *him*. Musk and sandal-wood, and something else that makes her knees go weak.

An ancient pulse of blood.

"Your family," Ehvy says as she watches him prowl closer. "This manor." She clears her throat and swallows the thick spit pooling in her mouth. "Rebecca."

"Ah." He rolls his head when he says it. His shoulders relax and a smile swims along his lips. "Rebecca."

Will stands over her, his body crowding hers, but she doesn't move until he takes another step forward, pushing her back. The only way to stop it would be to step around him, but her body craves his. Her lips long to feel his again, his hands roving her flesh. Yet her panic rises as he watches her move with a wicked smile on his lips. As if she's brushing close to the truth and it amuses him.

"Who is she? To you? What I could find says she died in a carriage accident," Ehvy sputters. Her words come out fast and sharp as she tries to reign in her thudding heart.

Her ass hits a table and she slides onto it, her feet leaving the floor as Will walks between her legs, trapping her there. The voice that existed at the beginning, the one warning her of all the bad things to come, stays silent just when Ehvy thought she'd hear it loudest. Now the voice is quiet and her knees part to allow him closer.

"The details are mostly true," he says as he brushes a piece of stray hair behind her ear, his other hand dancing fingers along her thigh. "But it wasn't a carriage accident that killed her."

"And your doppelgänger in the pictures with her? So many years between them, yet you—*he*—looks the same in every one. So does she." His thumb drags down her lower lip and Ehvy suppresses a shudder, her body pulsing for the man hovering over her. "I want to know how that's possible."

"What else?" he asks as his hand disappears underneath her nightgown and his fingers tease at her opening.

Ehvy chokes when he inserts one finger, then another, curving them inside her as she gasps with the movement.

"Tell me," he whispers in her ear as he trails his lips down its shell, moving over her jaw and down her neck.

"I found your family tree. William Sandridge's line stops. Ends. No one's used your family crypt in hundreds of years. The blood. I only see you at night."

Ehvy's breaths are short as he probes her, her hips bucking in rhythm with his movement as her knees spread wider. Will's finger trails down her shoulder under the thin silk strap of her gown; it drops, exposing her breast to him. The silence grows thick between them as he fucks her with his hand, his thumb grazing along her nipple. He holds her breast and takes the hard peak in his mouth, locking his teeth around it as he sucks.

Her hands grasp the edge of the desk, and she melts help-lessly under him, trapped and unwilling to escape.

"I've been dreaming about you for years, some nameless man in my head, until we met. I've been some lithe, pale-haired woman you fell on your knees for, another nameless creature in my dreams. Until I saw her in a portrait in your manor."

Sharpness rips across the tender flesh of her breast and Ehvy knows he's drawn blood. His tongue presses into the cut as he laps at it. All the while his hand works wonders in her cunt. Her pleasure mounts as he sucks and probes her, his hand grabbing her breast to hold it in place as she moves her body closer to him.

"What the fuck is happening, Will?" she pants, her vision speckling as her orgasm blooms, then crashes, sending her wailing over the edge.

Will's head rises from her chest, her blood on his lips as he pulls his fingers from her pussy and sticks them in his mouth. He stares at her, lapping her up all over again. His pajama bottoms tent, his cock straining for release. She expects him to laugh at her, tell her she's silly. That there are perfectly reasonable explanations for everything that's happened.

Instead, he wraps his fingers around the back of her neck and pulls her closer, his eyes fathomless, ancient history swimming in their depths. They're more alive than she's ever seen them, and she can't help but press her fingers into his jaw, the soft, shaven skin under her hand warm and inviting. His cock presses against her center, begging for entrance.

"I believe it's time for you to get those answers," he whispers over her mouth before he presses his lips onto hers. "Come with me."

Ehvy's heartbeat is a timpani inside her head. Blood whooshes as Will's waiting palm reaches to her.

Take it, a voice in her ear whispers as a flutter of blonde hair dances in the corner of her vision.

She's standing on a precipice as her toes cling to the edge. The enormity of the moment sits heavy in her bones. Will hadn't laughed at all the silly notions she said. He didn't whisper condescending things as he plunged his fingers into her sex. But perhaps that's coming. What he's going to show her will rip the rug out from under her.

Ehvy's mind has been playing tricks on her this whole time: the punchline of this long-running joke. Connecting dots that didn't connect. Seeing things that weren't there. Maybe Will is nothing more than an elaborate hallucination after all.

Fear wends its way through the mess she's become since meeting him. She should run. Escape into the night in nothing but what she has on.

Instead, she places her hand in his and allows him to pull her from the desk and lead her from his secret room. Her body sparks to life with his touch. An overwhelming sense of déjà vu makes her head spin. It feels as if all roads have led to this moment. None of this is a trick. How she and Will are drawn together and crave each other. How their bodies sing with each other's touch. All of this was simply an inevitability.

Fate, not chance.

Even as she questioned him, concern thick in her voice about *what* he could be, she still opened her legs. Let him slide his fingers into her. Allowed herself to be pleasured by someone who could be a monster. What does that say about her?

Her bare feet press into cold tile, pussy still pulsing from the orgasm he just gave her while her mind spins with thoughts of what he could show her.

Chapter Eleven

EHVY

"Hell is empty, and all the devils are here."

The flooring creaks under their feet as they walk and a pale, bare foot steps next to Ehvy. Shimmering silk flows between thin legs as the ghost of Rebecca takes another step, matching Ehvy's pace. She stares at the ghost's thin blonde hair as it settles over Rebecca's head and cascades down her back. Pert nipples press through the thin fabric, the darkness of her areolas shadowy beneath the pale silk. A smirk ties up Rebecca's mouth as her gaze flicks between Will's back and Ehvy's face. It's a knowing look that speaks of secrets Rebecca already knows and Ehvy is about to find out.

Words form on Ehvy's lips as she watches her boyfriend's dead lover walk beside her. "I'm not Rebecca."

The words are a whisper. So low Ehvy isn't sure if she said anything at all. A cackle rings through the dead night and Rebecca's smirk grows larger as blood drips over her lips and speckles her dressing gown.

Will looks over his shoulder. The specter next to her goes unnoticed as his gaze lands on her. "No, you are not." He steps closer and runs a finger along her forehead to brush the hair off her face. "You are so like her, but you are not her. A piece of her soul, perhaps. But you are Ehvy and I am not looking to remake you in Rebecca's image. I loved her with all of my being, but she has been gone for longer than you've been alive. I've lived long enough to know I must move on."

Unless he's playing into Ehvy's delusions, he just admitted everything she's suspected. Rebecca was *his* wife, not his ancestor's. They lived multiple lifetimes together for God knows how long.

Because they're vampires.

Her eyes flick to the space next to her and she stifles a gasp. Gone is the picture-perfect visage of a dead woman. Replaced by a skeletal face pointing in Ehvy's direction. Flesh drips from Rebecca's bones. Her silk nightgown is little more than bloody tatters hanging on putrefying flesh. Clumps of hair dangle listlessly from her scalp as the depthless voids of her skeletal eyes stare Ehvy down.

"Are you the earl?" Ehvy asks. Her lip quivers as her gaze goes fuzzy watching Rebecca's corpse rot. "The one who attacked the villagers?"

The story from the docent. That salacious tale from that buried website. The original owner of this land from a thousand years ago, who was accused of devilry.

Will smiles, a warm thing that flushes Ehvy's veins with heat, pulsing the apex of her thighs.

"My father," Will says, a hint of derision in his tone. "The result of gambling debts to the wrong sort and a deal with the devil gone awry when he tried to escape them. He figured if he could become stronger than the goons collecting his coin, there would be no more debt." A scornful smile flits across his lips as his gaze goes distant. "He descended the ladder of dark arts, seeking practitioner after practitioner who could help him until they pointed to a fellow hidden under luxuriant wealth and high walls in London. My father returned from that trip a changed man." He huffs. "Literally."

A skeletal hand dripping with muscle and torn-open veins reaches for Will's arm, a tarnished gold wedding ring on her finger. Bones clatter as the sinew holding her together disintegrates. A finger falls from her rotting hand and hits the carpeted floor with a light thump.

"He turned you," Ehvy mutters, hardly believing the words she's saying.

If all of this is true, what more is out there, lurking in the shadows?

"Eventually. Mother was in denial that anything was wrong until he attacked my sister. They all ran from the estate after that. All but me. The heir. They lived normal human lives. They had children. Grandchildren. Great-grandchildren. And so on. As you saw," he says with a nod to her.

The family tree. Most of the lines kept going—except for Will's. William's.

Ehvy tries to form words, but none come out. Rebecca's jaw scrapes against bone before it clatters to the floor, the lower half of her nothing more than a pile of bones under crumbling ribs. Will must know what Ehvy wants to ask. Can read it on her face if not in her mind.

"Rebecca was not for hundreds of years after that, was she? And she came willingly."

His thumb glances across Ehvy's lip, the corpse of his dead lover collapsing next to him with him none the wiser. A shuddering breath tumbles out of her mouth, a weight settling on her chest. The silence grows thick between them. All the information Will just dumped into her mind crashes and knots together. Just when the ringing in her ears couldn't grow any louder, he finally speaks.

"Please, come with me. Let me show you everything."

His words are a gentle breeze across Ehvy's face. The heat of his hand in hers is a balm, despite her information overload. Will's midnight blue eyes are nearly black in the low light of the corridor.

A piece of her soul, he said. Reincarnation. A recycled soul reused and repurposed for the modern world. In the corner of Ehvy's eye, Rebecca's spine collapses. The wispy hair-covered skull rolls across the pile of bones before tumbling to the carpet.

There is no denying it. Will has awoken something within Ehvy. Some dormant desire tucked so deeply into her DNA she didn't realize it was there. The lust, the blood, and the undying ache she has for the man before her are undeniable. Encouraged by an ancient attraction to an essence that is Ehvy's very being. And Will's. Like attracts like. There's a darkness to Will that calls to her shadows, just as her life ensnares him, pulling him ever closer.

Go, the voice whispers. The pile of bones at Ehvy's feet is gone save for a small red stain darkening an already red carpet. She longs to touch it. To see if it's fresh. Taste its coppery flavor. Thoughts that would have had her running from herself only weeks ago have her questioning why she hasn't thought of them sooner.

Because Will wasn't in her life to sift them to the surface.

She nods and squeezes Will's hand, encouraging him to keep walking. They carry on in silence until a familiar, threatening door looms before them at the end of the corridor. Solid wood. Metal locking mechanism. Desperate darkness on the other side.

The absence of Will's warm hand in hers leaves a chill across her skin as he walks toward the door.

"The dungeons," she mutters, her voice breathy as Will pulls the latch on the old door.

She expects it to squeal like a door in a horror movie, yawning wide to swallow the protagonist whole. Instead, its hinges are silent, the darkness of the dungeon waiting to wrap her in its arms.

Then it hits her—the smell of blood—and her eyelids flutter as she inhales. It's the most delicious thing she's ever smelled. A high, tinkling laugh echoes through Ehvy's ears. Ehvy swears she sees a peek of fangs through Will's luscious lips. Confirmation yet again of what he's already told her. Or her mind is playing tricks on her.

Fear simmers just below the surface. Apprehension. Anticipation. Conflicting emotions war inside her as the darkness stares back.

His heart is yours, the voice whispers. Ehvy can't help the weight of acceptance that settles on her shoulders as gooseflesh prickles her neck.

She knows. It's so very clear in every word, every movement, and every action he makes.

"Come, love. It's all the confirmation you need."

He tugs on her hand, but she remains rooted to the spot. Ehvy doesn't pull away, but her shoulders brace as she looks between the darkness and Will.

"Confirmation of blood." She glances at the door. "So much blood."

He smiles, his lips pulling back over his teeth to reveal his extended canines. Proof that Ehvy wasn't seeing things. She gasps as all her self-doubt—all her reason and logic—melts away to be replaced by the monster under the bed. And she's ready to crawl under the bed to greet him, despite her racing heart.

"Yes," he hisses as he tugs on her arm again.

The little resistance she was giving disappears as she steps forward. Delicate toes clench the carpet before stepping onto the cold stone that will carry her into her dark future. She moves as if floating, the chill of the stone under her feet barely making her shiver. The temperature drops as they descend, but the heat from Will warms her and the overpowering scent of blood drives her forward.

When they near a room, Will swings Ehvy in front of him and wraps his arms around her. His warmth pours into her, and she places her hands over his arms and digs her fingers in. Her back presses into his chest despite the horrors she keeps uncovering. Horrors that don't horrify her. Nothing about Will horrifies her.

"You're a bedtime story," she whispers.

Will smiles into her ear. "What sort of stories were you

reading before sleep?" His nose nuzzles her neck. "No wonder you dreamt of a creature like me."

She clears her throat as her eyes glisten. "This won't be nice, will it?"

Will moves his hands to her shoulders and pushes her toward the room. "It will not."

Terror shudders through her. It makes her knees shake despite how she tries to hold herself together. The things Ehvy has seen in her career are mere moments in her mind. Clinical studies and notes in a tablet, her mind automatically separates the gruesome scene from the human it once was. It's how she has moved through her job and the carnage she has seen. Despite it all, she steps through the door and a strangled cry erupts from her mouth.

Will is at the hanging man in a flash—faster than Ehvy can see him move—and she stumbles into the wall. Her hand finds her mouth while the other braces against the stone. The flayed flesh of the man's chest hangs open. His stuttering heart is visible as his innards pool at his feet. The lone candle flickering in the gloom casts waves of shadows across the glistening muscle of his heart as it struggles to pump.

Jesus Christ. The man's still alive.

Will reaches inside the cracked-open chest and runs his finger along the man's liver before sticking it in his mouth. Revulsion and desperation battle inside her as she struggles to beat back her growing desire. A desire for Will. A desire for blood. So much blood. Her gums throb with need as her growing nausea makes her swoon.

"You want answers, love?" He motions around the room. His feet splash through viscous puddles and kick a string of intestines out of the way as he paces. Blood clings to the hems of his pajamas.

"Rebecca was my love for five hundred years before that fucking witch's protective spell fizzled long enough for the villagers to get wise. She was out one evening while I was on business. The villagers incapacitated her with holy water and charms that even I knew nothing about. Then they eviscerated her and left her for dead in an open field. The sun finished the rest." He smiles a tight, watery smile as Ehvy's gaze flicks between the mutilated man and Will.

Pain and loss and horror wash over her as images flash through her mind. Ehvy's dreams of Will and Rebecca. The life they had lived. The love they had shared. The suffering they had caused. Even now, she finds the human part of herself growing quieter and quieter as her bloodlust blooms in the face of the disemboweled man. The nausea subsides as Ehvy crosses the last frontier in her battle for reason.

Will marches toward her. He reaches for her face and his bloody fingers draw gently down her cheek. Ehvy flinches at the touch, yet she melts into his body. The comfort of his nearness calms her shaking. As if he can block her from what's in this room and make it all okay.

"I know you are not Rebecca. You are Ehvy, but you carry her essence. Your profession—what do you think that's borne of?" He motions behind him. "Your dreams of Rebecca and I. How you eventually ended up here with me." He nuzzles into her neck, his tongue trailing along the sensitive flesh. "How you nearly come from the scent of so much blood."

A sob shudders through her chest and a tear trails down Ehvy's cheek. When Will pulls his face up, more tears track down her face and she closes her eyes to block out the world. His fingers graze along her skin as he smooths a piece of hair off her cheek. She doesn't flinch, but her chin quivers as more tears escape.

"Ehvy, please," Will begs as he presses his forehead to hers, his hands cupping her face. "Say something."

Reason finds a crack to slither through and fights its way to the surface. But it's not fear or sadness or revulsion at what's in the room with them. At what Will is. It's fury. Seething anger that he hid this from her. Something so important. So monumental. They shared so much, yet he kept this information close to his chest.

Tears choke her as she gathers herself. Tries to wrangle her emotions into something she can grasp. There are so many things she wants to say. But when she sucks in a ragged breath, snarls, and shoves her hands into his chest, his eyes widen as he stumbles across the blood-splattered floor.

"You've been hiding this from me? This was what was in your study when we met, wasn't it?" She yells as she motions to the dying man on the other side of the room. "You strung me along this entire time."

Her fury falters as his eyes flash black and his fangs distend as he rushes into her. Fingers squeeze around her neck as her back hits the wall with a thud, and Ehvy grunts with the impact. Instead of flailing and screaming, anger rears up. She digs her nails into his arms and tries to pull his hand away. Will doesn't relent and hovers his monstrous face over hers, his strength of ages holding her in place.

"When would you expect me to reveal this to you? That day? Perhaps on your first return trip? Or over dinner in

London? Tell me, Ehvy. When would have been more appropriate? And when would you have believed it?"

Ehvy tilts her chin up, holding his glare as if she has a chance of standing up to him. She doesn't care that he can rip her in half with one hand. She will not back down on this.

"Has this all been a lie? Have you been manipulating me? Used some kind of power over me?" She spits through clenched teeth and Will snarls, teeth bared and ready to strike.

"On your knees," he growls.

He releases her throat and Ehvy drops to the ground. Her knees crack into the stone as shock echoes through her body. His partially erect cock sits at mouth level, sheathed in silk. She looks from his face to his groin as equal waves of loathing and lust wash through her. No matter how much her mind demands she move, her body stays where it is—susceptible to Will's desires.

"That is the power I *can* have over you. And you will know it unless I make you forget."

"How do I know you haven't done that already?" she snarls while still on her knees with her lips pursed.

Ehvy can't even make fists under his control, and her mind swirls around all of the possibilities. Her cunt drips with need as she perches immobile on the dungeon floor. Blood licks her legs as the eviscerated body hangs just behind her vampire lover.

Everything about this is irrational, but acceptance settles into her bones. Will has irrevocably changed her, and she's on her knees begging for it. It goes against so much of who she is, but she would rip the pants from Will's body and fuck him now if she could.

"It would be like waking from sleep. Everything you did while under my persuasion you would remember, but know it wasn't you controlling your body." Will audibly swallows as his eyes lose focus. "It's what killed Rebecca. The witch's magic mimics that power and amplifies it. People shook off the fugue long enough to realize what was happening and took their chances with her. They won."

Will steps back and Ehvy's muscles relax. Movement returns to her body, but she remains rigid. Disappointment flutters in her chest, but also gratitude. He could have done so many things to her while she was under his power, and he didn't. From what he explained, everything she's felt—all of her growing desires and needs—is all her own driven by the seed of Rebecca planted deep in her soul's history.

Her meeting Will was never accidental. Merely an eventuality. Coded into her DNA.

Ehvy's hands press into his thighs as she pulls herself to her feet, holding his gaze all the while. Her eyes flick past him —eyeing the dying man—and glance back at Will. The muscles in her jaw twitch and tears well in her eyes, but when she opens her mouth, her voice is steady, if not soft.

"What does this all mean, Will? What happens to me now? You kill me?"

He cups her chin and presses their noses together, then their lips. Thoughts of fighting him well within her, but they quickly die out. Ehvy relaxes the slightest bit as their tongues tease each other and passion pulses between them. But she keeps herself firm. Not willing to give in to him just yet.

"No. Killing you is not something I desire. I want you to

live. I want you to be what you're destined to be," he says before he kisses her again.

"What I'm destined to be," she whispers back as she places her hands on his wrists and holds him tight. "A vampire. Like you."

The dying man moans, but neither of them pays him any mind as they hold each other's gazes. Her friends weren't wrong when they talked about how Ehvy was the darkness to their light. Until Will, those shadows wrapped a morbid career and interests in history that were displeasing to everyone but her. Relegated to dreams she could brush off as nothing more than the creations of her mind, Ehvy accepted the dead were her calling—stuck in a basement prying their secrets from their flesh.

Now Will has unlocked the vault and released what her life has been hiding from her.

"And if I don't want it?" Her voice chokes. She knows without hearing him say it what the answer is. "You won't just let me go on my way, will you?"

"You understand the danger in that," he whispers. "I couldn't..."

That should terrify her, yet she doesn't even quiver. Nothing about Will is terrifying to her anymore. Nothing about this situation. Fate has brought her here, and she accepts the hand she's been dealt. Deep in her heart, it makes more sense than the life she was living. Just scratching the surface of her potential.

"I should be furious with you," Ehvy says, her voice even and her hands warm on his arms. "I should tear you to pieces. The choice you've given me isn't a choice, and I should resent you for that."

She wants to rip him apart the way he's shredded her. From the inside out. Her gaze lands on the suffering man once again, and she wonders if he's a villain in this world's story. If not, she will make sure his suffering ends and that no more innocent people would follow. The sharpness of Will's cheekbones draws her attention, his glistening canines. The pleading in his gaze. He will do anything for her, and she will make sure of that.

He strokes a thumb along her cheek as her breaths grow even and deep.

"Now you know, love," he says as he glides his thumb along her lip and they part for him. "With this knowledge, would you have done anything different? Would you have never returned and gone about your life?"

Silence sits thick between them as her eyes rove his face and she mulls over his question. The answer rises to the surface of her mind: no. But with each passing second, fear trickles onto Will's face. He is anything but forgettable. Nothing in this world could make her forget him now that he's in her life. As a fantasy her mind concocted, easy enough. As a dream made manifest, impossible.

Just when the silence rings the loudest, Ehvy's lips part. "No."

Will pulls his head back and frowns. "No?"

Ehvy shakes her head. "I would make all the same decisions again. I would change nothing."

Desperate relief washes over Will as he crashes his lips into hers and pulls her to him. His hands find her ass as he scoops her up; her legs wrap around him as he pushes her into the cold stone wall. She fists his hair and pulls him closer, their bodies on the verge of melding together.

"What does this mean now?" she pants as Will's lips trail down her neck. "Will you make me like you?"

"If you'll allow me," he whispers into her warm flesh. His nose runs along the vein in her neck. "You won't be able to tolerate blood until then. Not in any meaningful amount."

His teeth nip at her skin and Ehvy gasps. With Will nestled between her legs, his hardening length pressing into her, she watches the mutilated man with hunger and desire. Yes, she will end his suffering. She will become like Will and they will fuck their way through a bloody eternity—but it won't be at the necks of anyone other than the deserving. There are plenty in this world who are worthy of the pain they inflict on others. That is how she will continue to speak for those who no longer have a voice.

Judge. Jury. Executioner.

"Do it," she says, her voice harsh and demanding. She looks down at him, no doubt in her mind. This is what she wants. "Do it, Will. Before I change my mind."

"You must die, love. Vampires transcend death by rising from the ashes more alive than we entered them."

His tongue trails along her skin and she shudders. She isn't dying for Will. She is dying for herself. To transcend into a greater being.

"Do it," she says again as her thighs squeeze him tighter.

Will nuzzles into her neck again—his fangs long and sharp—before he presses his lips to her soft flesh. Popping skin and Ehvy's cry pierces the dreary space as Will buries himself in her and draws deeply from the fountain of blood pouring from her body.

Ehvy moans under him as he drains her, her hips

writing against him as her strength fades. His thumb finds her nipple as her nightgown drops off her shoulder and exposes her to him once again. Little breaths flutter on her lips as he drinks and flicks the sensitive peak.

The weak throb of an orgasm builds, but there's not enough life left within her to bring it to fruition. The more Will drinks, the less connected to her body Ehvy feels.

As her heartbeat struggles to keep a rhythm, he takes his last few pulls from her vein and lowers her to the ground. Ehvy's heart falters. The room spins and swirls and her eyes lose focus.

The last beats of her heart thump through her chest as Will bites into his wrist—opening the vein—and presses it to Ehvy's lips. The last flares of life flash through Ehvy's mind. Beautiful Will with her blood dripping down his chin is the last thing she sees before her eyes close.

The weight of him on her lips is the last thing she feels before she disconnects from her body and there is nothing but darkness.

Chapter Twelve

WILL

"I do begin to have bloody thoughts."

The press of still-warm lips against his wrist keeps him anchored to the earth. Will pours himself into Ehvy —his life for hers—as he counts the seconds of her death. For one painful, horrific moment he thought she wouldn't accept. That she would walk away from him and into the arms of permanent death instead of becoming like him.

Her stillness is unbearable, but he remains motionless next to her. Waiting for her to rise anew.

Just as worry creeps into his thoughts, Ehvy's eyes snap open and a panicked gasp rips through the silence of the dungeon. Her eyes flit from side to side as they take everything in. Before long, her senses take over and she lashes out to Will. Chilled fingers wrap around his wrist and yank him closer before she buries her teeth in his flesh.

What was a slow drip before is now an incessant pull as

Ehvy draws from him. Each suck on his arm hardens his cock. She pulls away and he allows her the space to lie there. The initial transition is overwhelming—sights, sounds, and smells are a cacophony of intrusion as all her human senses heighten.

If Ehvy was smelling blood like she was before and responding to it as she did as a human, as a vampire, she wouldn't be able to resist. Blood lust will override whatever moral compass she had about the things Will has done, at least for now. The hunger is all-consuming. He will teach her to control it—to push it down so it's little more than a dull ache—but he will also allow her to have fun. If Ehvy as a vampire is anything like Rebecca, they will surely have fun.

She sits up and looks at him, reaching out to run her fingers over his lips. A waterfall of blood cakes her chin and chest, the silk of her nightdress ruined. Will smiles as he watches her adjust to her changed body. She looks like the Ehvy who first walked into his study, but inside she's a different beast entirely. The confidence of a vampire, the invincibility, changes a person when they come into this new life. If they're already inclined to that thinking, the shift gives them permission to live gluttonously, the world as their oyster.

Her knees bend and she pulls herself to her feet, not caring about the blood on the floor or the fact that her hair is now caked in it. She's never looked more beautiful to Will than she does at this moment. He places a hand over his cock, rubbing the soft silk of his pajamas against himself as he watches her move toward the mutilated man, each step a measured press against the bloody stone floor.

The silk robe flows over her shoulders and down her arms, fluttering away in a colorful trail behind her. She runs her fingers along her bare skin where the silk had been, shuddering at her touch. It's all so much—he knows. She will adjust to it. They have all the time in the world.

Will steps to the side so he can watch her. The slow, calculated movements she makes. He wonders if she's feeling her bones moving against each other. How her muscles shift as she raises her arm. Blood clumps in her hair, twisting it into knots at the ends, dripping down her back. He will enjoy bathing her later, scrubbing every inch of her as she luxuriates under his touch. Under the lap of water like a million tongues over her body.

She stares at her fingers and wiggles them before reaching out and placing her hand in the man's chest cavity. She drags her fingers along the exposed ribs and pokes at his beating heart. Her thumb grazes his stomach before her hand plunges into his abdominal space, burying herself in him. Unfortunately, the nearly dead man doesn't respond, but that doesn't seem to matter to her.

The body squelches as she pulls her hand out and stares at the blood covering her skin. Ehvy rubs her fingertips together, the blood slick, before sliding her fingers in her mouth. Her eyes roll into the back of her head as she probes her mouth, her tongue coming out and laving her palm. The blood disappears, leaving her hand a loving pink.

Her eyes roll to him, a finger still in her mouth, and she smiles, her teeth sharp. Ready to bite.

"My love," she whispers just before she plunges her hand back into the man and yanks out his heart.

The man chokes, his last sign of life, before going limp in the chains holding him. Ehvy sticks out her tongue and runs it along the heart before sinking her teeth into its meat. She savors the organ like the juiciest apple, blood running down her chin as her night dress hangs from thin straps at her arms, her breasts bare and covered in blood.

The heart slips from her hand as she turns to Will, her eyes fierce and needy as she prowls closer. The night dress gathers at her hips, most of her body exposed, with her delicious cunt remaining hidden, waiting for Will to bury himself within her.

Will's ready to lunge at her and throw her against the wall, but she stands in front of him in less than a heartbeat. Her eyes close for a moment as she shakes her head, the movement having sent it spinning. That will take some time to get used to. It took Will months to adjust when he first turned. At least now, in this modern age, speed is normal.

Blood-caked fingers tug at a string, untying the bow at his hips and allowing his pajama bottoms to drop to his ankles. His cock stands straight out and Ehvy grips it, stroking him with her blood-covered hand. As if he needs to get harder. His hands reach out and cup her cheeks, but she grins and falls to her knees on the blood-soaked floor.

Her tongue flicks out, licking blood from his tip before she plunges him into her mouth. Thick, wet lips wrap around his cock, her warm throat nestling his length as she takes him. The flat of her tongue runs under him as she laps up the blood, cleaning him of her mess. His cock hits the back of her throat, her lips at his hilt yet her eyes don't water and there is no gag reflex.

Ehvy licks the blood from his cock until it's clean, then keeps going, tightening her lips and sucking him to explosion. As if she knows when he's about to come, she stops and takes out his knees, dropping him to the floor next to her. She pushes him back to a seated position; the cold, dirty stone is of little concern to him as his eternal love crawls across his lap and places his head at her opening.

Drenched and ready, he slides in easily as she lowers herself onto him and grinds her hips. She moves like water, lapping at his body as he plays with her. Her rhythm and grace are amplified by her new vampire powers. His teeth find her breast, his tongue flicking her nipple before he takes a bite, sinking his fangs in and drinking her transformed blood.

Ehvy wails on top of him as blood runs down her body. When Will lifts his head, he knows her blood coats his chin. She drags her fingers through it and sticks them in her mouth, sucking the blood away as she fucks him.

Will wraps his arms around her back, pulling her close as she spreads her legs wider, settling him deeper within her. He groans into her ear as she rides him, her body writhing against him as his peak grows closer.

"Welcome to eternity, my love," he says as he grabs a nipple between his fingers and twists.

Ehvy hisses and arches her back while squeezing her core around his cock. Will shudders and presses his face into her chest. She wraps her arms around him and runs her thumb along his jaw before pulling his face up to meet hers. He gazes at her. Her beauty, her cunning, her intelligence. His lost love is still there, only now she's more. Ehvy is more than what Rebecca ever was, and Will hopes he will be enough for her. He will give her everything she could ever dream of, and he will watch her conquer the world.

Her hand slides down his chest and settles just over his heart. Fingers flick at his nipple, twist and pull, and Will sucks air between his teeth. Fingertips pad along his pectoral until pressure hits his rib. Flesh gives, tearing, and Will throws his head back and moans as Ehvy presses her fingers into his chest.

The pain is exquisite, his cock painfully hard as Ehvy grinds into him and her fingers shove their way through ribs while bones crack and splinter. His hands latch onto her ass and pull her closer, burying himself in her core as she moves deeper into him.

Ehvy curls her fingers around the beating muscle, grabbing his heart. Her jaw drops and she smiles, the tip of her tongue touching her teeth as her gaze wanders his face.

To die here would be an infinite irony, but at her hands, Will would allow it. If she lets him live, recovery will be painful, but it will be in her arms; he prays to the gods that she will fuck him to good health. Her thumb grazes the wall of his heart as it pumps wildly, anticipation and orgasm building in tandem.

Will groans as she settles her hand in his chest. She keeps moving on him and Will settles into the throb of pain and pleasure coursing through his body as it swells to climax.

"Look at me when you come," Ehvy says, throaty and seductive as she holds him to her, making a smile flicker across his lips.

The words alone make him explode, his body arching into her as she keeps hold of him, his heart and his cock hers for the taking. As he comes down from his high, Ehvy's hand still buried in his chest, she leans over him, her blood-covered face a welcome sight, and smiles.

"Now that I have your heart, and you mine, we will make the devils of the world cower at our feet," she says before she presses her lips to his.

They will indeed.

Acknowledgments

This fever dream of a book is the product of a literal dream (send help), lots of public encouragement, and many rounds of editing. *A Thing Divine* is proof positive that whatever idea you have, it's not too much. It's never too much, because there will always be someone out there looking for exactly what you've written.

Many thanks to my beta readers who helped me wrangle this story into submission, and to my first editor, Samantha Swart, who did not shy away from erotic horror like I thought she might. To my editors at Black Rose/Quill & Crow, Tiff, Lisa, Kayla, and Cassandra who embraced this story with open arms, fangs, fists, and all.

An ever-deep curtsy of a thank you to Fay, this gorgeous cover's designer who effectively crawled into my head and pulled the images straight from its depths. I couldn't have asked for a better cover. A big thank you to Alma and the Q&C PR team, Mel and Cyndi, for waving the ATD banner everywhere they could. I couldn't have gotten the word out without them.

Of course my parents get a big pat on the back for always supporting my writing no matter what it is, and they are more than welcome to buy all the copies for themselves and their friends as long as they don't read it. For the love of everything that is holy I want to be able to look you all in the eye again. Thank you. To my extended family and close friends who applaud me at every step, and to my husband who is possibly my biggest cheerleader (I love you, my dorkling), thank you. And to my cats who have bean-smashed their way across my keyboard any number of times during the course of writing and editing this book, you're jerks, but thank you for your love all the same.

A special thank you to the early readers who happened to see the first iteration of this book when it was still up on Wattpad. You guys made me feel less weird about writing what I was writing as I was writing it. Your ongoing support and bug-eyed comments meant the word to me.

Trigger Index

Addiction
Biting
Blood Play
Cutting
Destructive Fisting
Dub-con (vampire victim)
Evisceration
Gore
Gore Play
Graphic Sex
Knife Play
Light Choking
Light Stalking
Masturbation
Murder
Nipple/Breast Mutilation
Obsessive Love
Swearing
Torture

About the Author

Rian Adara is a multi-genre author who has a deep love of morally gray (or black) characters, writing with a hint (or a lot) of darkness, and varying levels of spice. She enjoys destroying her readers with her words and riling them up at the same time. And may or may not derive joy from creeping them out too. When she's not writing she's reading, papercrafting, taking moody photos, wrangling her cats, and spending time with her husband. The gothic aesthetic of New England will always be considered home, no matter where she lives. *A Thing Divine* is her first novel.

Thank You For Reading

**BLACK
ROSE**

Thank you for reading *A Thing Divine*. We deeply appreciate our readers, and are grateful for everyone who takes the time to leave us a review. If you're interested, please visit our website to find review links. Your reviews help small presses and indie authors thrive, and we appreciate your support.

Other Black Rose Novellas

The Dark Queen's Apothecary

Beyond the Grace of God

Printed in the USA
CPSIA information can be obtained
at www.ICGtesting.com
JSHW082110240824
68634JS00004B/157